River Wild

**FRANCES
MENSAH
WILLIAMS**

First published in this edition in Great Britain in 2021

Copyright ©2021 Frances Mensah Williams

The right of Frances Mensah Williams to be identified as the author of this work has been asserted by her in accordance with the Copyright, Designs and Patents Act 1988.

The characters and events in this book are fictitious. Any similarity to real persons, dead or alive, is coincidental and not intended by the author.

All rights reserved. No part of this publication may be reproduced, stored in a retrieval system, distributed, or transmitted in any form or by any means, including photocopying, recording or other electronic or mechanical methods, without the prior written permission of the copyright owner and the publisher.

A CIP catalogue record for this book is available from the British Library

ISBN 978-0-9569175-9-1

Typeset by Aimee Dewar
Cover illustration by Ashley Santoro

For Melissa, Maxine, and Thomas. Love always.

Also by Frances Mensah Williams

Imperfect Arrangements
From Pasta to Pigfoot
From Pasta to Pigfoot: Second Helpings

Marula Heights Romance Novella Series
Sweet Mercy

Non-Fiction

Everyday Heroes: Learning from the Careers of Successful Black Professionals
I Want to Work in Africa: How to Move Your Career to the World's Most Exciting Continent
Enterprise Africa: A Guide to Planning Your Business in Africa

Is love the price for living the dream?

Ambitious real estate agent River Osei loves her job and dreams of living in a home as beautiful as those she sells to her clients. Putting marriage to her artist boyfriend Cameron on the back burner, River's only focus is to hit her house fund target.

But River's plan is thrown into turmoil when she negotiates a sale to demanding music mogul, Donald Ayo. He is immediately taken with her, and she is equally taken with his house – a beautiful mansion in the luxurious gated community of Marula Heights. With Donald pressing for a deal that includes more than a house, River is forced to choose between the man she loves and a lifestyle she craves.

But living the dream isn't always what it seems and even the best fantasies come at a cost. Faced with the real-life consequences of her choice, River must learn that a house is not a home and love is not for sale.

Prologue

Her father chose the name River when he first held her in his arms because her dark, smudgy eyes instantly reminded him of the ribbon of greyish-brown water that undulated through the forests and farmlands of his hometown. He cherished the memories of those rare moments of solitude playing along the riverbank and escaping his five rowdy siblings.

River's mother, exhausted by her first experience of childbirth and secretly annoyed at her husband for ignoring her heavy hints to name their first child after her, had not appreciated the strange appellation.

'We don't know anyone with a name like that,' she observed tartly when River's father announced his choice.

'Well, then, she will be truly unique,' her husband had gently responded.

Undaunted, River's mother had exacted her revenge by choosing to give her daughter the pet name of 'Mama' and only reluctantly using River's given name when forced to deal with officialdom such as doctors and school teachers.

Giving the child such an outlandish name was probably why her daughter was so stubbornly independent, her mother would complain as the years passed, fed up of pacifying friends and relatives who made it their business to ask why at the age of thirty River still showed no inclination to settle into marriage. River's father, pretending to hear neither his wife's grumbles nor the pleas of his three sisters that he talk some sense into his daughter, would simply raise his newspaper higher, as if enlisting its support to block out their protests.

Occasionally, his mind would drift back to the riverbank in his hometown and the tranquil refuge it had provided, and he would sigh.

Chapter 1

River drew up to the tall gates and stopped the car. She jerked up the handbrake and reached for the iPad lying on the passenger seat, scrolling impatiently through Harvey's email to check the address. Yes, this was most definitely the house. She returned her gaze to the building clearly visible through the golden bars and couldn't prevent a low whistle escaping from between her lips. After almost five years of selling and renting houses she had seen her fair share of properties but even by the standards of the luxurious gated community of Marula Heights, this ultra-modern glass-fronted structure was something else.

One day, I'm going to live in a place just like this! The thought flitted through River's mind as she stared dreamily at the building and imagined the elegant luxury that lay behind its façade. She was startled out of her reverie by the strident double blast of a car horn and she cursed aloud at the sight of a gleaming silver Mercedes in her rear-view mirror. *This is Ghana, for God's sake. Who the hell arrives anywhere on time, let alone early!*

Earlier in the day, River's boss, Harvey, who was handling the sale of the property, had fled the office for home to deal privately with the consequences of eating highly suspect street food. Harvey's predicament had given River a rare opportunity to finalise the sale of a luxury mansion and earn herself a slice of her boss's commission. With the house viewing scheduled for two o'clock, she had deliberately built in time to familiarise herself with the layout of the property and go through the draft contract. But by arriving so inconsiderately early, Harvey's client had left her no time to prepare for the meeting.

River suppressed a sigh and rummaged in her handbag for the fob Harvey had tossed in her direction before scooting out of the office. She would just have to wing it and hope for the best. She pressed the button firmly and as soon as the gates opened wide enough to accommodate the company-logo-embossed Mini Cooper Harvey insisted she use, she shot through the gap. A glance in the mirror showed the Mercedes following and coming to a stop directly behind her. Unclipping her seatbelt, River flipped down the sun visor to peer into the tiny square of mirror, carefully fluffing the thick mane of natural curly hair that framed her face before checking the bronze gloss she had slicked onto her full lips before leaving the office. With Harvey having worked on this deal for so long and trusting her to make the sale, her first encounter with the famous Donald Ayo was *not* the time to look shabby. She knew from Harvey's frequent complaints that the man was a tough negotiator with an abrasive personality but despite her boss's grumbles and Donald Ayo's fabled reputation as a ruthless operator, River was curious to meet the well-known – and extremely wealthy – music and TV entertainment producer.

Gathering up her iPad and phone, River slung her precious Prada bag, one of the few indulgences she'd permitted herself from her house buying fund, over her shoulder and opened the car door. The moment she stepped out of the car's air-conditioned coolness and onto the gravelled driveway, the heat from the afternoon sun scorched her bare shoulders and tiny beads of moisture prickled beneath her carefully applied make-up. Resisting the urge to fan herself, River shielded her eyes with one hand and watched a man emerge from the Mercedes and stride in her direction. She barely had time to register the man's height, slim build, and well-cut suit before he was standing in front of her, a leather folder tucked under one arm and the other outstretched in greeting.

'Miss Osei, I take it,' he stated without preamble. Even though she was wearing heels he was still several inches taller, forcing her to stare up at him. His eyes were hidden behind mirrored sunglasses and his lips were unsmiling. 'Thanks for being on time.'

River squashed a flash of irritation at the patronising tone and pasting what she hoped looked like a convincing smile on her face, she returned his firm handshake. The lure of Harvey's promised commission if she closed the deal was strong enough to ensure she kept her cool.

'Harvey sent me a text to say he's unwell and that you'll be going through the final viewing with me?' His brusque tone showed little sympathy for her boss's plight and River bit back the sarcastic retort hovering on her lips. While Harvey could be a pain in the backside, he had slaved for ages to secure this gem of a house for his client and it wouldn't hurt the man to show a bit of compassion.

'Good afternoon, Mr Ayo,' she said pointedly. *At least one of us has some manners.* 'Please, call me River. Harvey has brought me up to speed on where things are,' she mentally crossed her fingers as she continued, 'and I'm hoping we can settle any minor concerns about the property and agree a deal today.'

His reaction to her name wasn't the usual response whenever she first introduced herself of 'Is River your *real* name?', she grudgingly conceded. Instead, he simply nodded and said, 'Excellent. And call me Donald.'

Hoping she was imagining that his grip was slightly longer than good manners required, River retrieved her hand from his grasp and then blinked as Donald slipped off his sunglasses and trained dark, deep-set eyes on her. His piercing gaze moved slowly over her face and then he grinned, the unexpected smile softening the hard planes of his jaw and revealing teeth that were almost too perfectly straight and white.

Disconcerted by the intensity of his inspection and the sultry afternoon humidity, River gestured towards the house. 'Shall we go in?'

'Please, take the lead.'

After the briefest hesitation, she nodded and hurried up a pathway lined with flowering shrubs and bushes. The spicy fragrance from colourful wildflowers tamed into neat beds that matched the geometric precision of the house lingered in the air as her pencil heels drilled into the fine, loose gravel. Hearing his footsteps crunch behind her, River frowned to herself, not quite sure what to make of Donald Ayo. After years of listing and showing properties to prospective clients, she was skilled at dealing with flirtatious men and usually found that a brisk tone of voice accompanied by selective deafness pushed even the most persistent back into their box.

And yet, while she could hardly accuse Donald of flirting, his piercing scrutiny and wolfish smile were decidedly unsettling. She desperately needed Harvey's promised commission to take her house fund closer to its target and she could only pray that Donald wouldn't make clinching the deal any more difficult than was necessary.

As River approached the house, she slowed down to appraise the meticulous landscaping and the unusual combination of whitewashed concrete and glass with an expert eye. Conscious of Donald close behind, she took extra care not to slip on the short flight of shiny, white-tiled steps leading up to a wide, shaded verandah packed with potted plants and mini shrubs in ceramic planters. Picking her way carefully through the mini forest to reach a set of double doors, River scrabbled in her bag for the house keys. After unlocking the door, she pushed it open and stood back, flashing her first genuine smile at her client.

'Please go ahead. If I'm honest, you know this house better than I do.'

Donald chuckled at her candour. 'That's a surprisingly frank admission. I was expecting the full-on sales patter.'

She was struck once again by the difference a smile made to his stern features and she stood back to let him take the lead. Donald stepped over the threshold and River followed, deliberately leaving the front door ajar. After the unfortunate incident while showing a persistently flirtatious buyer around a house – three bedrooms and a delightful flower garden – in Dansoman, she made a point of never closing the door when she was alone with a client. Although in that particular case it was the client who had beaten a rapid retreat when River delivered a swift double blow to his head after he'd grabbed her bottom, she still thought it prudent to leave an escape route handy.

Walking into the massive hallway, River stared around in shocked delight. *Oh my God!* This house was even more delicious than she had imagined. Huge picture windows and a magnificent glass-domed atrium let in the brightness of the afternoon sun, while high ceilings and white walls created a welcome coolness from the clammy heat outside. She walked slowly towards the centre of the hallway and caught her breath in admiration at the sight of a magnificent wide staircase that wound its way to the upper floor, its polished dark wood steps flanked by glass panels and topped with a chrome handrail.

The sound of a throat being cleared brought her back down to earth.

'Sorry,' River muttered. A flush of embarrassment crept up her face, but she couldn't hide her excitement. 'It's just that – well...' she struggled to find the words, and then rallied. 'This house is *gorgeous*! I'm not surprised you want to buy it. *I'd* snap it up if I could afford it and I've only seen the hallway.'

'Now that sounds more like the sales pitch I was expecting,' was Donald's dry response. 'Look, I've got another property to see this afternoon so can we get started? There are one or two things I've highlighted from my surveyor's report that I want sorted out before I agree to anything.'

Her smile faded as she watched him open his leather-bound folder and extract a couple of stapled sheets.

Another property? She would have bet her Prada bag that Harvey had no idea his client was considering other places. And how could anyone in their right mind *not* want to snatch up this incredible house, she wondered with a prick of resentment at the man's high-handedness.

Unaware of the glare River was directing at him, Donald's attention was on the document he was flipping through. 'With any luck, there's nothing here that's a deal breaker,' he said crisply. 'Let's start with the formal living room, shall we?'

Without waiting for a reply, he set off through the nearest archway, leaving River to hasten after him. As they moved from room to room, it was soon apparent that there were considerably more than 'one or two things' on Donald's list. The man was both annoying and a perfectionist, River decided an hour later as she added yet another item to his extensive catalogue of demands. Concentrating on Donald's nitpicking was even more maddening when she would far rather have been admiring the house. She always found her first viewing of a property exciting, but this house with its grand living spaces, high ceilings, graceful arches, and stylish white décor was truly stunning. The magnificent staircase led up to a floor with five enormous double bedrooms, each one with polished wooden floors, generous walk-in wardrobes and beautifully appointed bathrooms that set her heart singing with joy. *This* was why she loved her job. Nothing – absolutely nothing – could beat the experience of walking around a beautiful home.

With the tour concluded, they were back in the hallway when, to River's relief, Donald finally thrust his list back into the folder and snapped it shut.

'Right, I think that covers everything. Subject to the vendor agreeing to these stipulations, we could have a deal.'

It was clear from his tone the meeting was over, and River stared at him in dismay. 'Could have' was not the answer she was after. Harvey had been crystal clear: no agreement, no commission. Without a firm commitment today from Donald, her boss would take back his client – and River's cut from the sale along with him.

Not if I can help it! River flipped her iPad shut and faced Donald squarely with her arms folded firmly across her chest. 'Look, Mr Ayo, I think you should re—'

She broke off as her mobile trilled loudly. But before she could reach into her bag to turn it off, the strident ringtone announced, '*CAMERON ... BOYFRIEND!*'

Donald raised an eyebrow and River fumbled in her bag for the phone, mortified by Cameron's timing. She glanced up and caught an expression of exaggerated patience on Donald's face and her embarrassment immediately switched to irritation. Refusing to let the man's obvious displeasure intimidate her, River calmly tapped the dancing green icon on her handset and moved a few paces away.

'*Babe*! You're not going to believe—'

'Cam, I'm with a client. I'll call you back,' River abruptly cut short the words streaming through the line before Cameron could finish his sentence. Glancing over at Donald who was unashamedly eavesdropping, she suppressed a sigh and pressed the phone against her cheek.

'I'm so sorry, but I'll call you back as soon as I'm free. I promise,' she soothed, cutting off the call before he could protest. Cameron would not be happy at being dismissed in such a summary fashion, but this was business, and her boyfriend would just have to understand.

Returning to her client, River flashed her best professional smile. 'I'm sorry about that. As I was about to say, Mr— I mean, Donald, I really need to know today if you are committed to this deal.'

She adopted a brisk tone to emphasise that neither of them had time to waste. 'Let me be honest with you. It's very rare for houses to come up for sale in Marula Heights and this one is, well, it's *exceptional*. I don't know if Harvey's told you, but we have another buyer who's very keen to put in an offer and the vendor is getting quite impatient for a sale. So, quite honestly, if you *still* have doubts about going ahead...'

She let her nonchalant shrug finish her sentence and watched Donald's eyes narrow into slits. His expression screamed pure scepticism, but she held his gaze without flinching, leaving the unspoken threat hanging between them. *Two can play this game, Mr Big-shot music producer.*

They stared at each other in silence, neither one of them blinking, and she felt the familiar rush of excitement. If there was one thing River thrived on, it was negotiating. Whether that meant haggling over food items in the market or bargaining over the price of a property, she had long ago discovered that she was willing to say or do whatever was necessary to close a sale. Cliché though it was, the another-buyer-ready-with-cash ploy still achieved the desired result nine times out of ten. Nothing about her expression indicated that her pulse was racing or that her palms were damp with nerves, but this was always the crunch point – the moment when a client would either give in and make an offer or walk away and call her bluff. But as the silence lengthened, despite River's outward bravado, her stomach began to loop around in cartwheels and uncertainty crept in, her nerves growing taut with sudden apprehension. This was no run-of-the-mill sale and neither was the multimillionaire Donald Ayo a typical client. Harvey had been working on this deal for months and in a rare moment of self-doubt, River suddenly wondered if she had gone too far. Even contemplating the potential repercussions from the lie she'd just told Donald had River catching her breath. If Donald called her bluff and walked away from the property, she was painfully aware that Harvey would *kill* her – especially if his client told him why.

Then just as she thought her lungs would explode, Donald nodded. Without breaking eye contact he said slowly, 'Okay then, River, let's make a deal.'

Fighting hard to conceal the tsunami of relief flooding through her, she forced a cool smile. 'I like the sound of that. What do you have in mind? You know the asking price is—'

Donald cut her off with a dismissive shake of his head. 'I've already told Harvey what I'm prepared to pay and that's not up for debate. However, if you want a commitment from me today, I could give you a firm yes. On one condition, though.'

She frowned in bewilderment. 'But I've already agreed we'll sort out all the issues on your list. I can assure you everything you've asked for will be completed to the highest specifications.'

'I wouldn't expect anything less, but that's not what I'm talking about. My condition has nothing to do with the house.'

Suddenly Donald's expression took on a brooding intensity and River experienced the same unease that had gripped her when they first met.

'I'm sorry but I don't understand.' A sideways glance confirmed the front door was still open, and she gripped the strap of her handbag in readiness.

Donald's lips unexpectedly parted into a grin that revealed his impossibly white teeth. 'You don't need to look so terrified, River. You might actually enjoy it.'

She gripped her bag even tighter. Clearly relishing seeing her composure rattled, Donald chuckled heartily, the sound coming from deep in his throat. 'Okay, I'll put my cards on the table. I like your style. You're... how should I put it... *different* to the women I usually come across. You're certainly no pushover and I suspect you have a bit of a wild side to you.'

Where exactly is this going? Stunned by the change in the direction of the conversation, River could feel her accelerated heartbeat pounding in her chest. She wasn't afraid of Donald, but she would be a fool not to treat this man with caution. There was an almost savage air about him that the smooth businessman exterior didn't quite conceal, and the hypnotic stare he had fixed on her was setting her nerves on edge.

River blinked hard to break the spell and raised her chin defiantly. 'That's a weird thing to say to someone you hardly know. I think you've got entirely the wrong idea about me.'

'We'll see,' Donald shrugged. 'As I said, I'm ready and willing to make a deal, but on my terms. *I* will commit here and now to buying this house – if *you* commit to having dinner with me tonight.'

Chapter 2

'*No, he didn't*! I know you told him to go *straight* to hell! How did he take it?'

Even over the phone, Sly sounded aghast and River imagined his round eyes bulging in horror. When River didn't immediately reply, Sly pounced with the speed of a hungry cheetah.

'*River*! *Please* don't tell me you actually agreed to it. He sounds like a total sleaze!'

'Oh, come on, that's a bit much,' she protested feebly.

It was swiftly dawning on her that she should have taken a moment to think things through before ringing her best friend the moment Donald's Mercedes had disappeared down the road. She also wished she'd taken longer to consider his outrageous proposition and she mentally kicked herself for agreeing so readily. *I blame Harvey and his stupid commission*!

Sly maintained a pointed silence and River tried again. 'Okay, so maybe asking me out was a bit shady—'

He broke in impatiently. 'You *think*?'

She ignored the sarcasm and ploughed on. 'Listen, I did what I had to do to secure the sale. I need this commission. You know that either Ma or I will end up killing the other one if I don't move out of home soon. I had no choice – not really. Harvey wasn't going to give me a penny if I didn't close the deal today.'

Sly's response was a sceptical snort and River sucked her teeth impatiently. The last thing she needed was being made to feel worse than she already did. 'Look, my friend, just calm down, will you? I only agreed to have dinner with the man, not to sleep with him!'

'Who said anything about sleeping with anyone? Unless that's where *your* mind is going. I'm sorry, *my friend*,' Sly echoed her words mockingly, 'but anyone who resorts to bribing a woman to have dinner with him is either too old and ugly to get a date or is just plain tacky.'

'He's not old or ugly. I think he's in his forties...' *Ugh, shut UP, River!* She bit hard on her tongue to stop any more words slipping out. Having already lit the fuse, this was no time to add fuel to Sly's fire. Her best friend prided himself on being brutally honest and while most of the time she appreciated – or at least tolerated – his straight talk, this was not one of those times and she tried to change the subject.

'So, how's your day going? What's happening at the gallery?' she asked brightly. Sly loved hating his job as PA to Nelson Prah, owner of the city's largest art gallery. Despite declining three different offers of employment during the almost five years he had worked for Nelson, Sly was at his happiest when complaining about his demanding boss. But for once he refused to take River's bait.

'Never mind the gallery, lady. If there's nothing wrong with what you're doing, then I assume you'll be telling Cameron you're going on a date with a client for, you know, the money?'

River winced. 'Stop making me sound like some kind of – oh, crap! I totally forgot to call Cam back. He rang while I was trying to close the deal with Donald Ayo, and I had to cut him off... *Sly?*'

Her friend sounded like he was choking, and River clutched at her chest. 'Oh my God, are you okay?' she demanded anxiously.

'Did you just say *Donald Ayo*! As in *Start the Music* Donald Ayo? Oh my God, I *love* that show! He's brutal to the contestants with horrible voices but he's made Leah Peters a global superstar! Sis, you didn't tell me *he* was your client!'

River groaned inwardly, annoyed at her slip. The property industry was fiercely competitive and one of Harvey's golden rules was guarding the confidentiality of their client list. Even sharing a customer's name with partners or spouses was an absolute no-no in his book.

'Technically, he's Harvey's client and I shouldn't even have mentioned him. Just forget I said anything. And, yeah, of course I'll tell Cameron. Not that *he'd* care.'

'Ooh... am I sensing a little trouble in my River's paradise?'

River mentally kicked herself for yet another slip of the tongue. This was neither the time nor place to analyse the state of her relationship. But having inadvertently opened the door, she knew Sly wouldn't allow her to shut it without providing details.

'No, not really,' she said reluctantly. 'It's probably the five-year itch or something. It's just – I don't know. If I'm honest, it feels like we've fallen into a rut. Cam's obsessed with his painting and—'

'—you're obsessed with making money,' Sly interjected. 'I can see how that might be a problem.'

Ignoring River's protest, he added thoughtfully, 'Maybe it's time you made a decision about whether to take things to the next level or simply call it a day. I mean, the poor guy's always talking about marriage and you're always saying no. How long are you going to keep this up?'

'*Talking* about marriage isn't the same thing as a proper proposal! Anyway, I'm not ready to get married yet. No way on earth am I going straight from my father's house to my husband's house, and certainly not for Cam's awful bungalow. I want my own place first, at least for a while. Besides, I don't want to break up with him. I *love* Cameron. I just wish he were as attentive and romantic as when we first started going out...' she tailed off for a moment and then added with a tinge of resignation, 'I suppose it could be worse. At the end of the day Cam understands me, and I can be myself around him. And *he* wouldn't judge me for having a meal with a client to celebrate a massive sale. Unlike some people I know.'

The sun was beating down fiercely, and River dabbed at her damp forehead with the back of her hand and fanned her face. 'Sly, this heat is killing me. Let's talk later.' Cutting off the call, she retraced her steps up the driveway and back into the house.

For a few minutes, she stood motionless inside the silent hallway and soaked in the cool, serene atmosphere. This was quite simply the most remarkable house she had ever seen. Once Harvey had recovered from his stomach upset, he would take over the sales process and she would have no reason to come back here, she thought regretfully. Gazing up through the glass-domed ceiling at the clear blue sky, she wondered if Donald Ayo appreciated how lucky he was that he'd soon be able to call this beautiful place home.

* * *

River drew up to a set of traffic lights and tapped on Cam's contact number before putting her phone on hands-free and wedging it securely against the iPad on the passenger seat. Predictably for a weekday afternoon in Accra, the roads were heaving with traffic and if she had to sit in a long line of slow-moving cars, River decided, she could take the opportunity to return her boyfriend's call.

'Hi!' Cameron puffed, sounding distinctly out of breath as he answered the phone on the tenth ring.

'What's up?' she asked curiously. 'Were you running or something?'

'Yeah, I was in the studio painting. I heard the phone, but I couldn't remember where I'd left it.'

River smiled at the grandiose description. Cameron's 'studio' was the spare bedroom in the dated bungalow he had been renting for years. Located just behind the city's industrial area, the only advantages of the ugly but functional property were its large rooms with huge old-fashioned windows which afforded Cameron the space and natural light he needed to paint.

'Actually, I'm glad you called me back. I've got some news.'

Not only was there no hint of annoyance in Cameron's voice at her cutting off his earlier call so abruptly, River noted, but he sounded excited, or at least as close to excitement as her laid-back boyfriend allowed himself to get. The traffic lights changed to green and she put the car into gear and moved forward.

'That sounds—' River broke off with a curse as the taxi in front of her suddenly pulled into the side of the road, forcing her to swerve around him to avoid a collision. Muttering under her breath, she pressed hard on her horn and was even more infuriated by the taxi driver's casual shrug as she drove past him.

'What's going on? Where are you?' Cameron asked, sounding concerned.

'Sorry, babe,' River muttered. 'Some idiot taxi driver. I'm driving back to the office. I was showing a client around a property in Marula Heights when you rang, which was why I couldn't talk.'

Cameron's loud whistle pierced through the phone speaker. '*Marula Heights*! Kwame's cousin rents a house there and he never stops going on about the place. Well, well, my girl is going *up* in the world.'

Although still shaken by the near accident, Cameron's infectious chuckle brought a reluctant smile to River's face. She turned on to the highway that led into the city centre while her boyfriend warmed to his theme.

'Babe, I know how much you love fine houses. After I've sold my first – I don't know, my first hundred paintings, I promise I'll buy us a place there.'

More like five hundred paintings – and even that would only cover the deposit. The disloyal thought flitted through River's mind before she could help herself, and feeling guilty for doubting him, she injected a note of enthusiasm into her voice.

'I'll hold you to that! Okay, so go on then, tell me your news. By the way, it's nice to hear you sound so energised for a change,' she teased. 'Who knew *that* was possible, Mr Cool?'

'Ha ha. Anyway, you remember I lent Kwame a couple of paintings when he opened his restaurant and wanted some art to jazz up the place?'

River gave a noncommittal murmur while she concentrated on navigating a busy roundabout, and Cameron continued cheerfully, 'Well, Kwame hosted a party at the restaurant last night and one of the guests asked him about the paintings. It turns out she's an art buyer and agent and is always on the lookout for new talent. Long story short, she loves my work and asked Kwame to set up a meeting with me. I've checked her out on the internet, and she's connected to a bunch of art galleries and big-time art investors, and not just in Ghana. It would be incredible if she decides to represent me. Just imagine, babe, I'll finally get my career off the ground.'

'Cameron, you *have* a career,' River said absently.

'For Christ's sake, River! Do you seriously think IT project management is my *dream*? How many times have I said that I only take on those contracts to pay my rent?'

Taken aback by the vehemence in his voice, River bit her lip and felt another stab of guilt at her lack of enthusiasm. But as much as she hoped this time would be different, there was no denying the art world was notoriously difficult to break into and they had been down this road before. It wouldn't be the first time someone had shown an interest in Cameron's work, only to go cold or disappear after their initial excitement. Besides, River struggled to imagine any high-calibre agent worth her salt being seen dead in Kwame's no-frills beer and grill joint.

But then, hadn't that always been the difference between them? Cameron was the relaxed perpetual optimist while she… well… was not. All at once she felt unaccountably sad. Was viewing the beautiful house in Marula Heights the reason why she suddenly felt so restless?

When they first started dating, River and Cameron had laughingly described themselves as the perfect example of opposites attracting. River was the unashamedly ambitious go-getter for whom working hard, saving money, and spending smart was the guaranteed route to success. Having joined Premier Properties as Harvey's assistant a few years after graduating from university, River had been quickly promoted to the role of salesperson. After three years of long hours spent drumming up new clients and successfully negotiating rentals and sales of increasingly high-calibre properties, she had risen to the position of senior salesperson. Apart from the occasional designer indulgence, which River considered to be investments and therefore smart spending, she diligently saved her salary to buy the ultimate status symbol, her own house. When most of her friends moved on to rent houses and flats together, River had stayed at home, enduring the constant warnings from her mother and her three aunties, all of whom spent more time in the Osei family house than in their own, to get married before it was too late. Although they never properly spelled out what 'too late' signified, the accompanying pursed lips and ominous tones strongly suggested it was better for her not to find out. Whenever River wondered if her house fund was worth the risk to her mental health of maintaining such close proximity to her busybody relatives, she would lie on her bed and gaze at the beautiful houses pinned onto the vision board on her bedroom wall, dreaming of the lifestyle that came with living behind such luxurious walls.

Cameron's lifestyle, by contrast, was simple and essentially involved living off short-term and highly paid IT contract work while focusing on his art. Although her boyfriend was undeniably talented, he was also aggravatingly stubborn, resisting River's pleas to engage more actively in networking with the right people and promoting his work. Describing social media as a time-wasting chore, his mantra of 'the right thing will happen when the time is right' cut no ice with River who was much more of a 'make things happen' girl. After five years of supporting Cameron's dreams when his paintings showed no sign of ever providing him with a decent income, River was finding it a struggle to hide her frustration at his refusal to exploit his lucrative technological skills or defend his lifestyle to her exasperated mother. Cameron might believe in waiting for things to happen, but she was increasingly questioning a relationship that seemed on a fast track to nowhere.

'... *River*? Are you still there?'

The urgency of Cameron's tone penetrated River's gloomy thoughts and she forced her mind back to the conversation at hand. 'Sorry, I think the reception dropped for a moment. So, when are you meeting this agent, then?'

'This evening. Kwame said she's travelling in a few days and wants to meet up as soon as possible. Can you come with me? I know it's only an initial meeting but if she starts talking about money or contracts, well... you're the expert at negotiating and all that stuff.'

Tonight? River frowned in dismay at the phone as if it were somehow responsible for the words coming through the speaker. Having planned to casually slip a line into the conversation about having dinner with a client, how could she now tell Cameron she was putting dinner with a pushy multimillionaire over supporting her boyfriend at a meeting that could change his life? Her mind spun frantically in search of a credible excuse. *Tell the truth and shame the devil.* She'd lost count of the number of times her mother had fruitlessly scolded her for lying. But truth was a highly overrated concept, in River's opinion, and if she'd lived her life sticking squarely to the facts, she would never have sold a single property. She tussled mentally with her dilemma. Deliberately lying to a boyfriend who was even more of a stickler for the truth than Sly was regrettable but confessing her unorthodox bargain with Donald Ayo was clearly not the best idea.

'—*babe?*'

River drew in a deep breath and let the words spill out unchecked. 'I can't. I'm so sorry but Harvey's sick and I promised I'd go to his house this evening and help him with the paperwork for the Marula Heights sale. The buyer is insisting on exchanging contracts within three weeks and he's asked for a long list of things to be done in the house before he signs. I'm sorry but I honestly don't have a choice. If the client backs out, we'll lose a ton of money from the sale.' *Well, I certainly will if Donald changes his mind.*

'I'm sorry, too. I could really have used your support.' Cameron sounded so forlorn that River had to clamp her lips together to stop herself offering to cancel her fictitious arrangement.

Then his voice brightened again. 'Listen, don't worry about it, I'll be fine. So, what's wrong with Harvey?'

'The idiot bought *waakye* from some random street seller because he fancied a heavy breakfast. You would think he'd know better by now,' she scoffed, relieved to change the subject. 'He's lucky he didn't catch typhoid again.'

Cameron chuckled softly. 'Poor guy. Give him my best. Well, I'd better get back to the studio. I'll give you a call after the meeting and tell you how it went.'

River had arrived at the office and she drove into the car park and reversed the Mini expertly into a parking space. Before ending the call, she hesitated and then said quickly, 'Um, babe, it's probably better if we speak tomorrow. I'm not sure how long I'll be at Harvey's this evening.'

Feeling an unexpected pang of conscience at compounding her lie, River switched off the engine and gathered her belongings before hurrying into the office.

Chapter 3

'Mama, you look *beautiful*!'

River stood in the doorway of the living room and allowed herself to bask in the warmth of her mother's smile and her rarely bestowed approval. The black dress River had chosen to wear for dinner clung to her curves, but its demure mid-calf length and modest neckline clearly ticked the boxes on her mother's list. Donald's remark about her having a wild side still rankled and she had been deliberately understated in her appearance. A light dusting of powder, carefully applied eyeliner and a slick of lip gloss represented the sum of her make-up, while her thick curly hair was neatly twisted and pinned back with a sparkly black clip.

Moments later a frown inserted itself between her mother's eyebrows and her tone switched from joyful to gloomy. 'Look at all this beauty wasted on that jobless boy when you could be married to a respectable professional man and giving me grandchildren.'

Auntie Mansa, the youngest of River's father's three sisters, had been examining River silently and broke the awkward silence. 'You look so gorgeous, my dear.' She gave a wistful sigh. 'My waist was as tiny as yours before I had children.'

The frown on River's mother's face deepened. 'But, Mansa, what does your waist matter when you have children? Surely Sedom and Angela are much more important than your figure?' Her stern expression challenged the other woman to disagree.

'Oh, sister, yes of course! What is life without our children?' Auntie Mansa murmured reassuringly before flashing River a mischievous smile. 'I hope your boyfriend isn't taking you to KFC in that dress, hmm?'

River laughed and struck an exaggerated pose with one hand on her hip. 'Auntie Mansa, do you think I get this glammed up to eat fried chicken?'

'KFC is probably all that one can afford,' her mother sniffed.

River bit hard on her tongue and tried not to roll her eyes and invite a lecture on disrespecting her elders. No matter how many times she'd explained that Cameron was more than capable of making a decent income, her mother would simply insist that a man who didn't hold down a professional job like her accountant husband was only a short step away from the breadline.

'Brother!' Auntie Mansa commanded, directing her gaze at the silent figure in the corner of the living room. 'Look at your daughter – doesn't she look beautiful?'

River's father was burrowed deep into his favourite armchair and engrossed in a newspaper, and River smiled affectionately at the guarded expression that crossed his face as he slowly emerged from behind its pages. Unlike his wife and sisters, her father was a firm believer in keeping his opinions to himself,

'Hmm... yes, you look very nice, sweetheart. Enjoy your evening.' With that, he raised his newspaper and resumed his reading.

River's mother threw an exasperated glance at her husband before returning to her theme. 'Mama, you will not always be young and beautiful. No, don't give me that look – I am your mother, and if I don't say it, I wouldn't be doing my job. How long are you going to waste your time waiting for that man, eh? At this rate, I will die before I see any grandchildren.'

Unable to help herself, River huffed impatiently, 'Ma, don't be so dramatic. I'm not wasting anything on Cameron, and anyway I'm having dinner with someone else.'

Shut UP, River! Instantly regretting her slip as she saw her mother's face light up, River continued hastily, 'No, no, what I mean is I'm going out with a client. It's a business dinner, not—'

But the damage was done. Looking rapturous, her mother clasped her hands together and let out an excited screech. 'KOFI! Did you hear your daughter? She has a dinner date and it's not with the jobless boy.'

Not trusting herself to speak, River walked over to drop a kiss on her father's head and muttered goodnight to the two women as she left the room. Picking up her keys from the table near the front door, she hurried out to the welcome silence of her car.

* * *

'Please, madam, come this way.'

The waiter greeted her with a respectful nod and gestured for River to follow him. Having taken her phone number before departing Marula Heights earlier that afternoon, Donald had sent her a text a couple of hours later with instructions to meet at the hotel informally known as The Embassy, because its restaurant was popular with foreign diplomats working in Ghana. As River dutifully tailed behind the waiter, her eyes widened at the opulent furnishings. It was bigger than she had expected and the high moulded ceilings, dark maroon walls with gilt-framed paintings and subdued lighting reeked of sophistication. Although the room was bustling, the hum of chatter from the cosmopolitan crowd only created a low, genteel soundtrack. While she meandered between tables to cross the room, praying not to catch her heels in the thick carpet, she cast discreet glances around at the clientele but couldn't see a single face she recognised. Given this was one of the swankiest restaurants in the city, that came as no real surprise. Her friends were more likely to be found in affordable wine bars or hanging out in Kwame's beer and grill joint. She sniffed the aroma of rich food penetrating the air conditioning appreciatively. *Even the air smells expensive! One day I'll be able to afford all of this for myself*, she vowed silently.

Donald was seated at a table set for two in a mahogany-panelled booth and he stood up as she approached. When she walked up to him, he ignored her proffered hand and instead gripped her shoulders and kissed her warmly on both cheeks. He was in another expensive looking suit, this one a dark navy, with an open-necked shirt in the palest shade of pink.

'Punctual yet again!' he beamed. 'Didn't I say you're different to other women? Might I add that you look very elegant in that dress – and with your hair up.' He gestured towards the seat across from his and waited for her to settle herself before resuming his place. River smiled and forced herself not to react to the inappropriateness of his comment, trying hard to squash the sense of disquiet Donald Ayo generated within her.

The waiter was silently standing to attention and Donald picked up the drinks menu on the table and beckoned him forward. 'Bring me a Guinness – and make sure it's cold. And my lady here will have...?' He looked across at River enquiringly.

'Erm... I'd like a glass of white wine, please,' River said after a moment's hesitation. While it would be wise to keep a clear head, she sensed she would need something stronger than water to get through dinner with this unpredictable tycoon.

'Make that a bottle of the 2018 Pouilly Fumé,' Donald added peremptorily. He thrust the wine menu back at the waiter who nodded and hurried off.

River flashed Donald a cool smile and glanced around the room, trying not to look as intimidated as she was suddenly feeling. 'This place is very popular. How did you manage to book a table at such short notice?'

Donald shrugged. 'I'm a regular customer, so a reservation here is never an issue.' He rubbed his chin thoughtfully. 'As you grow to know me better, you'll find out that getting what I want is rarely a problem.'

The stare he directed at her was so intense she shivered, admiring his unapologetic self-confidence, but also repelled by his arrogant entitlement. Then she mentally pulled herself together. She wasn't here to provide Donald Ayo with an admiring audience, but to... *what, River? Why are you even here?* Suddenly overwhelmed by her surroundings, she pleated the linen napkin draped over her lap between her fingers and thought longingly of sweet, uncomplicated Cameron. With Cameron, what you saw was what you got, unlike the inscrutable music mogul sitting opposite her, and in that moment River longed to be transported to Kwame's joint and enjoying kebabs while negotiating contracts with Cam's potential new agent.

As if sensing her unease, Donald leaned forward and said quietly, 'Thank you for joining me for dinner tonight, River. I know you probably felt pressured into agreeing to my er... proposition, but I'm very intrigued by you and I want to know you better. And who knows, you might even end up *liking* me.'

He cocked his head to one side with such a cheeky smile that River couldn't help giggling. Immediately, the tension between her shoulder blades eased and she leaned back in her seat with a wry smile. *I'm here now, so I may as well enjoy some good food and what sounded like very expensive wine.*

'That's more like it,' Donald nodded approvingly. 'You have a beautiful smile, and you should laugh more often. Now then, tell me about yourself.'

'Oh my God,' River groaned. 'That sounds like a job interview question.'

'Fair enough,' Donald chuckled. 'Okay then, how long have you been working for Harvey?'

'That's not much better,' she grinned cheerfully. 'Let's see, it must be almost six years now. I had a couple of jobs after I graduated, but nothing I really enjoyed. Then Harvey offered me a job at Premier. He's been really good to me and gave me a chance to move into sales, which is what I've always wanted. It's hard work but, well… I just love selling property.'

The waiter's arrival with their drinks caused a brief lull in the conversation and once their glasses had been filled and the server had moved away, Donald raised his beer mug and clinked it against the wine glass she held up in turn.

'Cheers, River. It's a pleasure to be here with you.'

She smiled and took a long sip of the chilled aromatic wine, sighing with pleasure as she tasted its delicate fruity tang.

Donald watched her with a satisfied smile. 'I'm glad you like it. It's one of my favourites. We can order in a few minutes but first tell me more about you. Why do you enjoy working in real estate?'

Feeling a little more at ease, River stared appraisingly at the man sitting opposite her. Her eyes were drawn to the tiny diamond nestling in his earlobe and the glint of a thick gold chain visible through the open neck of his shirt and her gaze slowly wandered down to the fancy wristwatch peeking through the sleeve of his jacket. When she returned her gaze to Donald's face, he was looking straight at her and she flushed at his quizzical expression and dragged her mind back to his question.

'I love absolutely everything about real estate,' she said with a light shrug. 'I'm obsessed with looking around houses and curious about how people live and what a property says about a person. I also get a real kick out of negotiating and getting the best deals for my clients, whether they're buying or selling.'

River was so caught up in the conversation that it was almost a shock to see the waiter appear to take their order. She hadn't eaten since lunchtime and feeling a touch light-headed from the wine, she didn't protest when Donald ordered the chef's tasting menu for two without asking her opinion.

'I promise you'll enjoy it,' he assured her as the waiter moved away. 'Now, then, where were we?'

The courses that followed were as delicious as Donald had promised, and River tucked into a flavourful seafood bisque, succulent fish and chicken dishes, and a peppered steak that melted in her mouth. Along with the food, she was finding the company much more pleasant than she'd anticipated. Donald appeared content to listen and prompted her with questions throughout the meal, while the wine kept her tongue sufficiently loosened to ensure no awkward silences.

'It must be wonderful to eat like this whenever you like,' River sighed as she watched the waiter clear away their used plates. She must have sounded more wistful than she realised because Donald chuckled and shook his head.

'You're not exactly a starving orphan,' he pointed out. 'You're well educated with a good job and I'm sure you could afford meals like this if you wanted. It's important to enjoy the good things in life, River, otherwise what's the point?'

She dabbed at her lips with the white napkin embossed with the hotel's logo and pondered on his words as she looked around the plush restaurant. Donald had a point, and maybe her obsession with saving for a house was preventing her from fully enjoying life. Now she had conquered her initial trepidation, River was thoroughly enjoying the luxury of her surroundings and, she had to admit, Donald's company. There was something seductive about the air of authority he projected and despite the rumours she'd heard about his business tactics, she couldn't help feeling a sneaking admiration for his reputed ruthlessness. As the evening went on, she also found herself increasingly comparing Donald's go-getting attitude to Cameron's lack of urgency and silently wondering if her mother was right about her wasting her time with Cam.

'The reason I don't eat at restaurants like this is because I'm saving up to buy my own place,' she said eventually.

Donald raised an eyebrow. 'So, you still live at home?'

She nodded and sipped the wine she hadn't noticed the waiter topping up. 'It's not easy, believe me. My family is always getting into my business and my mother nags me constantly to get married.'

'Ah yes, "Cameron… boyfriend,"' Donald murmured, taking a swallow of his beer.

River looked at him uncertainly, but his bland smile gave nothing away and she continued, 'Yes. He's an artist and we've been going out for years but neither of us is ready to get married. Well, at least, I'm not,' she added, wondering whether to blame the wine or Donald's endless questions for sharing such personal information with a virtual stranger. She was vaguely aware that Donald had offered hardly any details about himself but after consuming more than half the bottle, her brain was too fogged to care.

'Ah, you see! I *knew* you had a wild side,' Donald grinned. 'Most of the women I meet are desperate to settle down and have kids.'

'Don't get me wrong, I don't have anything against marriage...', she tailed off with a sigh as she momentarily contemplated married life with Cameron. 'I'm just not ready for that kind of commitment until I've achieved my own goals.'

'There's nothing wrong with being ambitious, River.' Donald caught the waiter's eye and he swiftly brought over their dessert menus.

River took another sip of her wine. 'You try telling my mother that. According to her, my younger sister's boyfriend is far too respectful to propose to *her* until I get married. Which, of course, lets Kojo off the hook. Not that the boy has any intention of proposing since both he and Sefa are barely out of uni.'

River was engrossed in the extensive dessert menu and trying to choose between white chocolate cheesecake and mango-flavoured tiramisu when she heard a lilting voice coming from behind her loudly exclaim, '*Donald*! How very nice to see you.'

'Hello, Nina! This is a pleasant surprise.'

River watched as Donald tossed his napkin onto the table and stood up to embrace an attractive woman wearing a short lime-green dress which revealed extremely shapely legs. With a smile, Donald gestured towards River.

'Nina, let me introduce you to my companion, River Osei.'

Not quite sure how to feel about Donald's description

of her status, River remained seated and offered the woman a courteous smile. The smile vanished when seconds later Nina was joined by a new arrival. *What the hell is Cameron doing here?* Shocked, River stared open-mouthed at the sight of her boyfriend standing next to Nina. Having assumed Cameron's meeting would be in Kwame's restaurant, The Embassy was the last place she would have imagined running into him.

River's face burned with mortification as Cameron's stony gaze moved from her face to the almost empty wine bottle on the table and then back again.

Nina was oblivious to the silent exchange and urged Cameron forward. 'Donald, this is Cameron King. He's an incredible artist I've just discovered.'

Despite her shock, it was all River could do to stop herself from screaming, '*You* didn't discover him, you silly cow. He's been mine for *years!*'

Other than a raised eyebrow followed by a quick glance at River, Donald gave no indication that he knew who Cameron was, and he held out a hand to exchange a brisk handshake.

'We've just finished dinner,' Nina continued, her voice bubbling with enthusiasm. 'And it's going to be the first of many because I'm now Cameron's agent. I cannot wait to get his work out into the world. Honestly, Donald, he has such an original way of using colour, and his perspective is so sharp and – well, I'd better stop, or I'll just go on forever.'

Donald eyed Cameron appraisingly. 'Well, in that case, congratulations. Nina has a fantastic eye for talent and if she's in your corner, you'll do very well.'

Curious to gauge Cameron's reaction to Donald, River chanced a quick glance up at him. From the nerve pulsing at the side of his jaw, she knew immediately that her boyfriend was absolutely livid, and yet when he spoke, he sounded deceptively calm.

'I can only agree with you, Mr Ayo. From the little I've seen so far, Nina's amazing, and of course, her track record in the art business is super impressive. But what I really like is how refreshingly honest and upfront she's been with me, which I think is incredibly important in any relationship.' He smiled at Nina who was looking at him with a smile so wide that River felt sick. Without breaking eye contact with Nina, Cameron added softly, 'I feel very lucky and I'm honestly so excited about where our partnership will go.'

Is he deliberately trying to hurt me? River wondered resentfully. Cameron's carefully worded compliments about his new agent were a less than subtle dig at his girlfriend who had been anything but honest about her plans for the evening. River's eyes zeroed in on Nina's hand still clasping Cameron's arm and she fumed silently at the woman's lack of professionalism in her over-familiarity with a client.

Nina pulled Cameron even closer against her until River's head felt like it was about to explode, but Nina's attention was on Donald as she winked. 'You'll be among the first to know when I've put together Cameron's first exhibition and I promise you will *not* want to miss out on investing in his work.'

With that, she tugged gently on Cameron's arm and waggled her fingers in farewell. 'We'll leave you two alone to finish your dinner, but I'll be in touch soon, Donald. Oh, and it's nice to meet you... um, River, was it? Wow, is that your *real* name?'

Chapter 4

'So, basically, you lied to me.' Cameron's gaze was fixed on River as he carefully wiped his paint-stained hands on a faded rag. His eyes, deep pools of melted dark chocolate that had drawn her in from the first moment she'd laid eyes on him, were ringed with exhaustion and his chiselled features tight with barely suppressed anger.

'I'm sorry,' River said humbly. The conversation was going from bad to worse and Cameron was even more furious with her than she had feared. He had ignored her phone calls all day and with Harvey back at work and breathing down her neck to ensure that all the modifications Donald Ayo had demanded were underway it had been well after six o'clock before River had finally escaped the office. After a further hour navigating rush-hour traffic, she had arrived at Cameron's house fully intent on smoothing things over between them. Unfortunately, her stumbling explanations appeared to be cutting no ice.

River took a deep breath and tried once more. 'Look, like I said, I'd already promised to have dinner with Donald when we spoke on the phone. It's just that... well, after what you said about needing me to come with you to meet Nina, I didn't know how to say no without sounding like—' Afraid of worsening an already bad situation, she broke off, and he helpfully finished off her sentence.

'—like a woman lying to her man because she'd prefer to entertain a client to guarantee her cut from a good deal.'

River glared at him, her anger at the insinuation behind his words briefly overcoming her contrition. 'That is *not* fair!'

'Why? Is there anything I've just said which isn't true?'

'Cameron, *please* understand. Yesterday, Donald Ayo committed to buying the most amazing mansion which I would never, under normal circumstances, have been given the chance to sell. There is absolutely no reason for you to be jealous because I was having a celebratory dinner with a client.' She conveniently forgot her raging jealousy of Nina the previous evening. '*You* were having a business dinner too, weren't you?'

'Which *I* had told you about,' he countered pointedly. 'And, if there was nothing wrong with what you were doing, then why lie to me? How the hell do you expect me to trust you when you literally see nothing wrong with bending the truth when you feel like it. You know I can't stand dishonesty!'

Cameron tossed the rag onto a paint-encrusted table covered with half-squeezed tubes of coloured oils and a collection of paintbrushes. His T-shirt and black jeans were splattered with paint and he had clearly been at his easel for hours. Despite her anxiety about the turn their conversation was taking, River couldn't suppress the flutter of longing brought on by the sight of Cameron's muscular arms, taut stomach and strong thighs, and she sighed, wishing he would stop fighting with her and take her into his arms. What *was* this obsession Cameron and

Sly had with always telling the truth? Being honest was highly overrated and it almost always guaranteed that someone would get hurt.

But her boyfriend was clearly waiting for a response and River shrugged. 'It was wrong of me not to be honest with you, and I'm sorry about that. But, honestly, this deal is going to pay me the biggest commission I've ever earned. Which means that I'll have enough in my house fund sooner for a deposit and I can finally move out. Getting the opportunity to make this sale was a chance in a lifetime and I didn't want to jeopardise it. It was *only* business with Donald, I promise! And I insisted we went somewhere public,' she added lamely.

'River, I've told you a hundred times that if you want to leave home, you can come and stay here.' He ignored her exasperated groan and continued doggedly, 'Okay, so I might not be your mother's ideal choice of a husband, but if you're worried about upsetting her by living with me, we can get married. I'm prepared to do whatever makes you happy.'

How many times must we have this conversation? River stared at him in silent frustration. She could tell from the stubborn set of his jaw that he still refused to understand why she kept turning down his offer to move in with him. But even leaving aside Cameron's less than romantic rationale for marriage, River simply couldn't imagine living in his bungalow. This functional, ugly house was not to her taste and she pushed away the image of the house in Marula Heights that suddenly popped into her mind.

'I'm sorry but I can't.' Exasperated by Cameron's stubborn resistance to improving both their lives, River's attempts at diplomacy vanished. Sweeping an arm around to encompass not only the studio they were in, but the entire bungalow, she burst out, 'I just don't want to settle for – for *this*!'

The moment the words emerged, Cameron's expression darkened, and she immediately wished them back. A prickle of unease crawled up River's spine and she watched in trepidation as his eyes narrowed in scorn. She had come here to apologise but she only seemed to be fuelling her boyfriend's anger.

'Well, I'm so sorry this house isn't good enough for Princess River!'

'I didn't mean—'

'Oh, come on, River,' Cameron broke in impatiently. 'I know it's not like the posh mansions you find in Marula Heights, but it's really not that bad, is it? Just be honest.'

The trouble with honesty, River thought bleakly, was that once you started on top of that hill, there was nowhere else to go but down. She took a deep breath and let her words tumble out. 'Cameron, maybe *you're* happy renting this place but honestly, look around you. The walls are damp, the roof leaks, the fittings are dated, and the entire décor needs a refresh. Yes, I know if you make the landlord fix it up, he'll increase the rent, blah blah blah. But, okay, if this is what you want, then let's *really* be honest. How the hell can you live like this? And how can you expect *me* to move into a place that's in this state?'

Pausing to draw breath, she decided to take her chances. 'Look, it's not like you don't have options, Cam. If you focused on your IT skills instead of—'

She broke off in alarm as Cameron hurled a paintbrush he had just picked up onto the table with a loud thwack before turning on her with eyes blazing.

'For the hundredth time, *I AM AN ARTIST*!' he bellowed. 'What don't you get about that? My "IT skills"' – he raised his fingers into sarcastic air quotes – 'have only ever been about paying my bills.'

Equally frustrated, River shouted back, '*Fine*! But then let's be clear that *I* can't live here. If I moved into this place, it would be like me admitting that this is the best I'll ever do.'

Cameron gave a loud snort of annoyance. 'Oh, come on, River! Have a little faith for once. This is *not* how it's going to be forever, and you know that. I already have almost enough paintings for my first exhibition and I've now got Nina Arthur representing me. *I* have faith that I'll make it so why can't you have faith in me?'

'Cameron, it's been *five years*! Don't you think it's time you at least have a better back-up plan? If you had a proper job instead of just taking on work when you need money, you'd have more cash to invest in your painting... and your house.' She glanced around the room, not even trying to conceal her distaste.

'Jeez, River, you sound just like your mother!'

She gasped as his words stabbed right into her heart with the force of a steel dagger. Of all the things he could have said to her, this was almost the worst. And yet, buried beneath her outrage was her fear that maybe Ma had been right all along. River would have died rather than give her mother the satisfaction of saying so, but if Cam really was the right man for her, he surely wouldn't expect her to begin their lives together in this dingy house? She didn't expect Marula Heights – or, at least, not yet – but she knew she was worth more than this dismal place.

Fighting back the tears that were prickling behind her eyes, River stared at him sadly. It was time for honesty about where things stood between them. 'Cameron, we've had this argument countless times and it looks like we'll never agree. So, where exactly are we going?'

Cameron looked as wretched as she felt, but his gaze didn't falter. 'I don't know,' he sighed. 'But I think it's obvious that wherever we're going, we're not going to get there together. It destroys me to say it, but if you don't want this,' he mimicked her earlier gesture, 'then you don't want me. Because *this* is who I am, at least for now. Even if you have no faith in me as an artist, *I* do, and believe me, I'm not letting anything get in the way of that. So maybe let's just call it quits now before this gets even harder.'

He turned back to the table and shifted a few tubes of paint into a semblance of order. Then without looking up, he said quietly, 'You should go.'

River stared at him in disbelief. '*Cam*! What are you saying? You *can't* be serious! Look, I was wrong to lie to you and I've apologised. But you can't just end things because I don't want to move in with you.'

'So, then what else is there? I've offered marriage and you're not interested. If I have the nerve to even mention us having a child together, you look at me like I've got two heads!'

River groaned aloud. '*Where* exactly do we fit children into our lives? You tell me how we're supposed to take care of a child when your lifestyle is so focused on painting and I'm living at home and nowhere near reaching the goals I've set for myself.'

'Not everything in life has to be planned down to the last detail,' he said impatiently. 'It wouldn't hurt you to learn how to go with the flow a bit more instead of expecting everything and everyone to fit into your non-negotiable timetable.'

She flinched but held her ground. 'Look, we obviously have issues we need to resolve but—'

'But what? You're right, we've had this argument too many times already and neither of us ever gives an inch because we each want what we want. We're done here, River. I don't know what else there is to say.' He sounded as calm as if he were reasoning with a stubborn child who would eventually see sense. Picking up a small brush from the table, he dipped it into a pot and brushed feather light strokes onto the canvas resting on the paint-spattered easel.

'*Cameron!*'

Without taking his eyes off the painting, he shook his head. 'You need to leave, River.'

Stunned by the speed with which her relationship was disintegrating, River's eyes flooded with tears which she swiftly blinked away. There was no way in hell she was giving him the satisfaction of seeing her cry, she thought angrily. If he could be so – so *callous*, she fumed, she would show him she didn't give a damn either. Snatching up her bag, she turned on her heel and marched out of the house without another word.

That's what comes of being bloody honest, River

thought bitterly as she climbed back into her car and started the engine. Why do people claim they want complete honesty and then they're not happy when they get it?

Dashing away the tears spilling onto her cheeks, she blindly steered her car out of Cameron's driveway and on to the dark road ahead.

Chapter 5

'*Mama*! Mama, Let me in!'

River pulled her bed covers over her head to muffle the sound of her mother pounding on her bedroom door. The disastrous scene with Cameron had been followed by a sleepless night and an awful day at the office. Earlier that morning, a new client had pulled out of a house sale which River had been nurturing for weeks, followed two hours later by a call from another client confirming she'd found a new apartment through a rival broker. In between the bouts of bad news, River had struggled to keep at bay the tears which threatened to escape whenever she thought of Cameron. Now, physically exhausted and emotionally drained, the last thing River needed was her mother rubbing salt into her wounds.

Suddenly the pounding stopped, and River cautiously poked her head out from under the light bedspread. Any hope of being left alone swiftly vanished as another voice joined the chorus.

'*River*! It's me. Open the door.'

With a sigh of exasperation, River bounded off her bed to unlock the door. Despite the five-year gap between them, she and her sister were close and while her mother would eventually have gone away, Sefa was another matter. The word 'no' simply didn't feature in her younger sister's vocabulary and she would have camped outside River's door all night if necessary.

River turned the key in the lock and immediately returned to her bed, and seconds later her sister burst through the door closely followed by their mother.

'Mama! Are you sick? Why are you in your bed at this time?' her mother demanded as she marched into the room. 'It's not like you to miss dinner. What has happened?'

Sefa dropped onto the corner of her sister's bed and her long braids swung loosely as she tucked a leg under her, her brow ridged with concern. 'What's going on, sis? Is it just Ma being a drama queen again? She seems to think you're having a mental breakdown because you missed a meal.'

Ignoring Sefa's dig, her mother added earnestly, 'Auntie Essie brought some of her special jollof rice that you love so much.'

'Ma, I'm fine,' River protested. 'I've had a long day and I just need some quiet time to myself.'

Looking unconvinced, her mother pursed her lips and folded her arms. 'Just because you are tired doesn't mean you don't eat. Especially Auntie Essie's jollof. My daughter, I am neither deaf nor blind. You were crying half the night and then today, look, you are refusing to eat. Therefore, something is wrong.'

River caught Sefa's eye and, despite the cloud of misery swirling around her, River couldn't help the wry smile that crept onto her lips. 'Honestly, Ma, you sound like a TV detective about to announce the killer. I'll eat later, okay?'

Sefa tucked an errant braid behind her ear and stared at her sister curiously. 'Why *were* you crying? Is it Cameron?'

River signalled frantically with her eyes but Sefa simply shrugged. 'Ma's going to find out anyway, you know what she's like, so you might as well tell us. Did you guys have a fight?'

River rolled her eyes, wondering yet again what she had done to deserve relatives with so little respect for boundaries. She looked from one pair of enquiring eyes to the other and exhaled noisily. 'I give up! There is no such thing as privacy in this house, is there? I can't wait to buy my own place where no one bothers me if I decide to stay in my room so I can have ten minutes of peace.'

Her outburst caused no discernible shift in the expectant expressions on the faces staring at her and River sighed again. She dropped her gaze and traced a fingernail lightly over the pattern of her bedspread and then said quietly, 'Since you're both so desperate to know my business, Cameron and I broke up. There, that's it.'

When neither Sefa nor her mother spoke, River looked up, mystified by their silence. Sefa, to her credit, looked horrified by the news. Which was more than could be said for her mother, who made no attempt to hide the wide smile spreading across her face.

'But, my daughter, what is there to cry about? You made a good decision! I told you that boy was wasting your time.'

'It wasn't my decision, Ma,' River said bitterly. 'He's the one who did it.'

Sefa's eyes grew even wider. '*Nooo!*' she breathed. 'What the *hell*? What did you *do*?'

'Why does it have to be me that did something?' River

shot back, incensed at the assumption that she was the one at fault.

'Because Cameron's crazy about you and I can't see him doing the breaking up unless you did something very, *very* bad,' Sefa retorted.

River's mother sat down heavily on the other side of the bed and her smile faded into a puzzled frown. 'Ah, Mama, let me understand. Are you saying that jobless boy broke up with *you*? But – but he was fortunate that you even minded him. Why did he do that?'

Faced with two sets of interrogating eyes, River broke. With a disconsolate sniff, she returned her gaze to the bedspread and said carefully, 'he was upset with me for not being, well – you know, entirely honest about something, and now he says he can't trust me.' She thought it best to leave out the details of Cam's offer to move in with him and the accusation that she was as shallow as her mother.

Again, there was silence. River looked up to see Sefa's lips quivering and she sucked her teeth in annoyance. 'Sef, it's not funny!'

Her sister giggled unrepentantly. '"*Not entirely honest*"? Come on, sis. You mean you told one of your whoppers and got found out. It must have been a big one if he finished with you. *What* did you do?'

Reluctantly, River related the story of Donald Ayo's request, carefully omitting his name this time, and the unexpected meeting with Cameron and Nina at the restaurant.

'Mama, how many times have I told you to tell the truth and shame the devil,' her mother clucked sternly when River came to the end of her story. 'You did not need to lie to the boy. Imagine his embarrassment at seeing you having dinner with another man.'

River stared at her mother in disbelief. This was the closest to sympathy for Cameron her mother had ever expressed. Great, she thought bitterly, now he's broken up with me, you finally have a kind word to say about him!

Sefa kicked off her flip-flops and settled herself more comfortably. Crossing her legs, she rested her elbows on her knees and stared intently at her sister. 'River, I still don't get it. Cameron knows you can be… erm… shall we say, flexible with the truth from time to time, and I'm sure he was piss— um, sorry Ma, upset at seeing you out with another man. But you guys have been together for years. He must know it didn't mean anything.'

'Ye-es,' River conceded reluctantly. Sefa was clearly not going to let this go and there wasn't much point in any further prevarication. 'But then I also said I didn't want to move into his house… and I didn't want to marry him.'

Sefa whistled loudly. '*Wo-ow*! *Now*, I get it! But, sis, if you don't want to be with him, why are you so upset?'

'Because I didn't want to break up with him!' River wailed. 'I was just trying to get Cam to understand that I'm not prepared to settle for living in that God-awful— sorry, Ma, I mean, awful bungalow. I want a nice house, I *deserve* a nice house and if he can't be bothered to do what it takes, well then maybe I *am* better off without him!'

Sefa's gaze turned to the wall opposite the bed where River's vision board held pride of place. 'Look, I know you're really serious about this house business but is that really a reason to give up on Cameron? Kojo's always saying what an amazing artist he is, and you never know. I mean, he could make it really big one day and—'

'Don't you think I've told myself the same thing a hundred times?' River cut in impatiently. 'I understand he loves painting and I'm sure one day he'll make it as an artist. I know Donald really rates Cam's new agent, but however good an agent Nina is, there's no guarantee she can make him a commercial success, and even if she can, it's not likely to happen overnight. The point is he could be making great money *right now* in IT. I mean the guy is in huge demand and he charges a massive daily rate. But all he cares about is his art, not about me...'

Her voice thickened as tears rolled down her cheeks, and Sefa sighed and shifted up the bed to drape a comforting arm around her sister. 'Shh, it's okay, sis, don't cry. Maybe it just wasn't meant to be. You both want different things and I know it's hard but... it's probably for the best.'

After a few minutes and just as River's tears subsided, her mother, who had lapsed into uncharacteristic silence, gave a loud exclamation before quickly covering her mouth with her hand.

River and Sefa exchanged puzzled looks as the older woman shook her head. 'Oh, *Sefa*! Whatever will you tell Kojo?' Her voice was heavy with sorrow. 'The poor man has been waiting for your sister to marry so he can also ask you.'

Sefa hooted with laughter. 'Ma, you are something else! I'm only twenty-five and Kojo and I have no plans to get married. In fact, I'm thinking about applying for a bursary at work to do an MBA. There's a course at the University which I could do part-time over three years.'

'Three *years*!' her mother exploded, looking the picture of anguished misery. 'Why don't you just kill me now. *Haba*! When will I ever get my grandchildren?'

Sefa shook her head and gave her sister a gentle hug before sliding to the edge of the bed to fish for her flip-flops. 'Seriously, Ma, you're getting upset for nothing.' She slipped her feet into the sandals and looked up with a cheeky grin. 'This is the 21st century and it's not a case of either 'MBA' or 'MRS', you know. If Kojo and I decide to get married, I can actually do both at the same time.'

Her mother rose to her feet without a word and carefully smoothed down her cotton caftan. Walking to the door, she reached for the handle and then turned around to pin Sefa with a dark stare. 'You think I am upset for nothing? Hmm, okay, you just continue to follow your sister.'

She paused to give River a sympathetic smile before returning her gaze to her younger daughter. 'See her now – thirty years old and with no husband or boyfriend. Even that jobless boy was better than nothing!'

Chapter 6

'River, did you hear what I just said?'

'Hmm... sorry, Harvey.' Slumped back in her chair, River sighed and dragged her attention back to her impatient boss. Harvey had been on the warpath all day after losing his bid to handle the sale of a large commercial property and this was not the place or time to mentally relive the awful scene with Cameron. It had been over a week since their bust-up and with no word from him, she was slowly facing the painful reality that her boyfriend had meant what he'd said, and their relationship was over. To make matters worse, her head felt thick and foggy after her extended drinking session with Sly the night before. She had been desperate to escape Sefa's kindly but annoyingly solicitous enquiries and the repeated demands of her three aunties to detail the specifics of the break-up conversation for their analysis. Her mother's incessant deep sighs and sorrowful glances had finally tipped River over the edge, and she had dragged a reluctant Sly away from his sofa and his favourite *Start the Music* TV show for a night of purposeful drinking.

With Kwame's restaurant automatically out of bounds on account of him being Cameron's best friend, River and Sly had ended up in a wine bar near the beach knocking back shots until three in the morning when Sly had unceremoniously pushed her into an Uber. Now, after three hours sleep and with a heart as heavy as her head, River tried to pull herself together while her boss fumed about Donald Ayo's last-minute revision of a clause in the sale agreement. When Harvey finally ground to a halt, he thrust a manila envelope in her direction.

'So now you need to take these updated contracts over to him asap' – Harvey always pronounced it '*a-sarp*' and River had never had the heart to correct him – 'He'll meet you at the property.'

Surprised, River jerked bolt upright and frowned. 'Why me? Donald Ayo's *your* client. Can't we just send them by courier if you're too busy?'

'Because he asked for *you*,' Harvey said bluntly. 'Listen, the man has just spent nearly twenty million cedis on a property in Marula Heights. So, if he says he wants you to bring him the contracts, then that is what he gets.'

'I didn't think being pimped out was part of my job description,' River grumbled. But even as she spoke, she reached for her bag knowing from long experience that arguing with Harvey was a waste of time. Reminding herself she would see her promised share of the sale commission once the agreement was signed and contracts exchanged offered a degree of consolation. As did the realisation that it was another chance to view the gorgeous Marula Heights house before Donald Ayo took ownership.

River stepped out into the bright sunshine and walked towards the car park, slipping on her sunglasses with hands still shaky from the vodka she'd consumed the night before. With no viewings scheduled for the day, she was dressed casually in black jeans and a white vest top which accentuated her curvy bust and tiny waist.

She started the engine and rolled down the windows to dispel the heat inside the car. Why did Donald Ayo want to see her, she wondered? Other than a brief call on her part to thank him for dinner, there had been no further communication with the music mogul since their dinner at The Embassy, confounding Cameron's accusations that Donald had designs on her.

Fortunately for her lingering hangover, traffic was lighter than usual for a mid-week afternoon and River arrived at the Marula Heights property within half an hour. The gates were open, and Donald's Mercedes was in the driveway. She parked her Mini Cooper behind it, recalling their first meeting and smiling faintly at how their positions were now reversed. Grabbing her bag and the envelope containing the contracts, she glanced in the mirror and gave her hair a quick fluff before stepping out of the car.

'*River*! Come on up.'

Slamming the car door shut, River turned around to see Donald leaning against the porch wall, his gleaming smile visible even at a distance. She walked up the pathway to join him and just as he had done at dinner, he grasped her shoulders and kissed her on both cheeks. Releasing her, he took a step back and openly raked a critical eye over her.

'You're looking well, but I have to confess I prefer women to wear dresses.'

Taken aback by the blunt declaration, River bit back her instinctive reply and thrust the envelope at him. 'Harvey said you wanted me to bring you these for signing,' she said shortly. Between her hangover, the humidity, and Donald's inappropriate commentary, she could feel her temper fraying at the edges. 'If you don't mind signing the contracts now, I can get them back to Harvey before he leaves the office for the day.'

Ignoring her outstretched hand, Donald sauntered through the open front door and then stood aside to usher her in. 'All in good time. Come on in... I thought you might like to check on the work that was done since you're the one who arranged everything.'

River's desire to see around the mansion again easily trumped her irritation at its new owner, and she tucked the envelope under her arm without comment and walked through into the bright hallway. Pushing her sunglasses up into her hair, she looked around in delight, experiencing once again the strong sense of connection to the elegantly designed house she had felt on her first visit. After dutifully admiring the string of minor repairs and modifications Donald had insisted upon, she followed him back to the hallway where he turned to face her squarely.

'Look, River, I know I can be quite particular,' he started, and she raised an eyebrow. His stern features broke into a rueful grin and he continued, 'Okay, I can be very particular, but I asked for you today instead of Harvey because I wanted to thank you personally for your efforts in getting all this done. You were right, by the way. It's all been finished to the highest standard.'

'You're very welcome, and it's been a pleasure to serve your needs.' She trotted out her standard phrase and held out the papers once again. 'I have a pen in my bag if you need one,' she offered.

Donald reached into his jacket pocket and extracted a solid silver pen which was a far cry from the black plastic biro she'd been about to lend him. He took the envelope and walked over to a low cabinet against the wall, laying out the sheets and carefully reading through the document. River approached quietly and watched as he gave a satisfied nod and then she held her breath as he hovered his pen over the line marked for his signature.

He looked at her and his deep-set eyes narrowed, causing River's heart to sink. *What now?*

'I'd like to ask you a favour,' he said abruptly. 'I'm signing the contract anyway, so there are no conditions this time.'

'Oka-ay,' River replied warily. 'What's the favour?'

'I'm attending a charity awards dinner on Saturday evening and I would really like it if you came with me.'

River blinked in shock. With her mind fully engaged on the contract that would deliver her biggest bonus to date, this was certainly not what she had been expecting.

Without waiting for an answer, Donald scribbled his signature on the document with big bold strokes and drew a line underneath it with a flourish. Repeating the process with the duplicate copy, he gathered the papers together and slipped them back into the envelope before handing it back to her.

'It's been a pleasure doing business with you, Ms Osei,' he said solemnly. He put his pen away and held out his hand.

River grinned with relief and shook it firmly. 'The pleasure is all mine, Mr Ayo.'

'Now, will you answer my question?'

River detected a hint of uncertainty in his voice and pounced on the first chink she had seen in Donald's confident armour. 'Only if you answer mine first,' she said thoughtfully. 'Why did you really ask for me? You already have the house keys, and we could have sent you the contract by courier.'

Donald hesitated, and then shrugged. 'Because I wanted to see you again. I was curious about what happened between you and "Cameron boyfriend" after that very awkward end to our dinner. Tell me, did you manage to smooth things over?'

River ducked her head and focused on the toes of her black canvas shoes.

'River?'

His voice was unexpectedly gentle, and she looked up and shook her head dumbly. Whether it was tiredness from the lack of sleep or the effects of the vodka on her emotions, River's eyes suddenly flooded with tears and a sob escaped before she could hold it in.

Without a word, Donald reached for her and wrapped his arms tenderly around her. Far too upset to feel embarrassed, River allowed herself to lean against him, grateful for the comfort and hoping she didn't soak his white linen shirt. His hands rubbed her back gently and after a few moments she gathered the strength to push away from him, feeling curiously bereft of his warmth when she did. He reached into his pocket and extracted a handkerchief which she accepted gratefully. After dabbing at her eyes with the spotless linen square, she grimaced at the streaks of mascara left behind.

'Better?' he asked gently.

She nodded. 'I'm sorry, that was really unprofessional of me. I—'

He placed a warm finger on her lips and shook his head. 'No apologies needed. It was my fault. I should have minded my own business.'

The touch of his finger made her lips tingle, and she broke away, pretending to smooth back her hair. This was a very different side to Donald Ayo, and River felt guilty for misjudging him. Instead of the brusque, arrogant tycoon she had observed to date, Donald was showing himself to be warm, sensitive, and kind-hearted.

'I'd really like you to accompany me tomorrow,' he said smoothly. 'Come on, River, take a chance. You'll have a good time, I promise. And just think of all the people with deep pockets you could meet there. You know how important it is to network among the right people – that's how you steer high-net-worth clients to your company.'

Although River's instinctive reaction was to refuse the offer, the prospect of bringing new business to Premier Properties was hugely tempting. Selling houses to the rich people Donald surrounded himself with would propel her into the big leagues and bring enough money to fund the lifestyle she deserved. But her last date with Donald had led to the end of her relationship with Cameron, she reminded herself. If she agreed to a second date, and this time voluntarily, wasn't she signalling to Donald that she found him attractive? Even if he hadn't made it clear he was interested in her, River wasn't naïve enough to imagine he was asking her out for the joy of helping Harvey build his property business.

Donald was watching closely while the different thoughts chased through her mind, and River turned and walked towards the window, hoping some distance would help clear her head. On one hand, she loved Cameron and was still hoping that he would calm down and have a change of heart. But, on the other hand… She looked up at the beautiful skylight and her mind flew to her vision board and the dream house waiting for her if she could only find the money.

'Say yes, River wild,' Donald murmured persuasively. 'What do you have to lose?'

What indeed? All at once, Good River was swept aside by Practical River and she eyed Donald speculatively, relishing the power of this wealthy man begging for her company. Cameron had made it clear he saw no future for them, and it was time to look out for herself. Before River could argue herself out of it, she heard herself agreeing.

Donald smiled with satisfaction and she added lamely, 'Just to be clear, you do know I'm still with Cameron? Or at least I will be when he stops being so stubborn.'

Her declaration made no apparent dent in Donald's self-assuredness. Gesturing for her to lead the way out of the house, he remarked dryly, 'I don't know which one of us you're trying to convince, River. We both know that if you really wanted Cameron, you'd have said yes to him a long time ago.'

Chapter 7

River was walking hand in hand with Cameron along a beach illuminated by an orange-red sunset when Sefa burst into her bedroom and bounded onto her bed, immediately shattering the dream.

'Wake up, sis!' There's a car downstairs with a delivery for you, and the driver says you have to personally sign for it.'

River struggled upright and glanced blearily at the clock on the bedside table. 'What the hell, Sef!' she mumbled, crushed at the abrupt intrusion into what had been a highly enjoyable dream. 'It's not even ten o'clock, and it's my Saturday off!'

'Well, do you want the delivery or not?' Sefa demanded. 'The man is waiting and Ma's not happy he wouldn't let her sign for it, so be prepared for her to be extra nosey.'

River grumpily adjusted the silky scarf knotted around her head and tossed aside the bedcovers. Slipping on her dressing gown, she disappeared into the adjoining bathroom to quickly brush her teeth before coming back into the room for her slippers.

'Oh, and watch out, the aunties are here,' Sefa called out after her as River stomped down the stairs.

The courier was waiting on the front porch when River opened the door, still too drowsy to notice her gown had fallen open to reveal her tiny vest and shorts. Scrawling her name at the bottom of the delivery form, she took the large box the man handed over with a cursory word of thanks and shut the door.

'Mama!' River's mother emerged from the living room and into the hallway. 'What is it? Have you ordered something special? That foolish man wouldn't let me take it for you.'

'Ma, I've literally just been given this box,' River protested, blinking the sleep out of her eyes, and reluctantly relinquishing the sunset-beach dream with Cameron. 'I haven't ordered anything, and I don't have any idea what this is,' she added with a nod at the package in her arms.

Sefa was on her way down the stairs and stopped halfway to sit on a step. 'Go on then, open it. Ma won't leave you in peace until she knows what it's in there, and now I'm dying to see what it is.'

River sighed inwardly at having to deal with such drama so early in the day and wished for the hundredth time for her own house far away from prying familial eyes. Forgetting Sefa's earlier warning, River carried the package into the living room and then stopped dead as three pairs of eyes turned in her direction.

Before River could utter more than a word of greeting to her aunties, her mother, who had been following close behind with Sefa, nudged her impatiently in the ribs.

'Mama, hurry up and open it. We are all waiting.'

'What's going on? What do you have there, my dear?' Auntie Mansa's voice was high with curiosity.

'Mansa, someone has sent Mama a package. It came by car,' River's mother announced.

'Ooh, I love surprises!' The plump woman sitting next to Auntie Mansa heaved herself off the sofa with a loud grunt and then clapped her hands as excitedly as a child.

'Essie, move out of the girl's way!' The admonishment came from a tall, thin woman sitting upright on a wooden stool with her legs neatly crossed at the ankle. Flashing an appreciative smile of thanks at Auntie Frema, the eldest of her father's sisters, River dropped the box on top of the mahogany sideboard. The women gathered around and there was a collective holding of breath as River ripped the tape away impatiently and wrestled the package open. She peeled back white tissue paper to pull out a frothy confection of red sequinned lace, and when she shook it out to reveal a stunning strapless gown, the women gasped in unison.

'*Bloody hell!*' Sefa pretended to cough as her mother glared at her. 'I mean, wow! But if you didn't order it, who did?'

Laying the dress on the sideboard, River fished out a small envelope at the bottom of the box stamped with the logo of a well-known fashion designer. Tearing it open, she slipped out a stiff card with black handwriting and her eyebrows shot up as she read the words.

'*River!*' Sefa pressed her impatiently, 'Who's it from? Oh my God, did Cameron send it to say he's sorry?'

Shocked into silence, River could only shake her head. With an exasperated tut, Sefa snatched the card out of her sister's hand and read it aloud. '*I'm looking forward to seeing you wear this tonight.*'

Sefa looked at River with narrowed eyes. 'Okay, I'd bet anything this isn't from Cameron! What *have* you been up to?'

River smiled weakly. 'Nothing. It's – he's a client and um...' Her voice ground into silence as she surveyed the range of expressions around the room.

'Is this the same client you were having dinner with when Cameron caught you?' Auntie Mansa was the first to break the tense silence.

River nodded and snatched the handwritten card back from Sefa, raking over the words again as if they would provide more clarity with a second reading. What the *hell* was Donald Ayo playing at by sending her clothes. Just because she'd agreed to accompany him to the charity dinner didn't mean he had the right to dictate what she'd wear!

'My dear, who exactly *is* this client?' Auntie Frema's deep voice intruded into River's indignant thoughts. 'If someone is sending you expensive gifts, I think we should at least know his name.'

River looked up at her curious relatives and suppressed the urge to tell them to mind their own business. Why could no one in her family – apart from her father – observe boundaries? And yet knowing it would be fruitless to even try keeping a secret from the inquisitive bloodhounds staring at her, River muttered reluctantly, 'Donald Ayo'.

Sefa shrieked and jumped up and down with glee. '*Nooo*! Donald *Ayo*! You mean, the famous music guy? Sis, he's a millionaire! Oh my God, you've struck *gold*!'

Clearly unimpressed by her younger daughter's crowing, River's mother frowned doubtfully. 'But, Mama, is it proper for a man to send you clothes when you are not even engaged?'

Auntie Mansa snorted loudly before River could reply. 'Sister, don't you *know* who this man is? He is very famous! Angela makes me watch his show every week. Please don't complain when we have been waiting *years* for our daughter to find a man like this.'

'She's right, my sister,' Auntie Essie echoed. 'The man is showing his intentions. How many people would send such a gift? And by car, no less? He knows she is a princess and deserves to be treated like one.'

Feeling very un-princess-like in her nightclothes with an old scarf wrapped around her head, River gathered up the dress, her mind still in a whirl. She might not yet own a wardrobe of designer clothes, but she would have found something suitable for tonight's event. As much as she recognised Donald's generosity, she didn't appreciate his presumptuousness in deciding what she should wear. She thought back uneasily to the time he'd ordered dinner without bothering to ask her opinion and squirmed at the memory of him eyeing her in her jeans before pronouncing his preference for women in dresses. Had she made the right call in agreeing to go out with him? River felt a sudden shiver of apprehension run down her spine. Donald Ayo was a different animal altogether from Cameron who had always regarded her as his equal, and she was fast coming to realise that with Donald she was dealing with a rich – no, a *very* rich and strong-willed older man who was used to getting exactly what he wanted. And now he had made it clear that what he wanted was River, how would she be able to stand her ground?

***

River put the finishing touches to her lip gloss and tilted her head to check her reflection in the mirror. The dark smoky shadow and the lashings of mascara made her eyes appear huge in her face. Her well-defined cheekbones were highlighted with discreet bronze shading and her full lips were tinted a deep red to match her new dress. A visit to the salon for a manicure earlier in the day had transformed her short colourless nails into perfectly polished scarlet ovals.

Dressed only in her underwear, River glanced over at the lace gown suspended on a hanger hooked over her wardrobe door and felt butterflies of excitement flutter in her stomach. Donald's audacity might be maddening but the lace dress was gorgeous. It was also very tight, and she had skipped lunch and eaten only a few slices of fruit earlier in the evening to be able to comfortably zip up the unforgiving fabric. Her favourite black heels waited patiently by the wardrobe and her sparkly black evening purse lay on the bed, ready to go. The dress would be slipped on at the last minute to avoid any accidents.

River returned her gaze to the mirror and reached for a hair pick to fluff out her freshly washed natural curls. The car Donald had arranged to collect her was due at any moment and she felt increasing trepidation at attending an event so prestigious she would normally only have glimpsed it on television. Her nerves were so taut that she flinched when her phone unexpectedly burst into life.

'CAMERON ... BOYFRIEND!'

The comb dropped from fingers that suddenly seemed

to lose their grip and River froze, her heart pounding as she stared blankly at the handset lying on her dressing table. She was so shocked that it took several rings before she pulled herself together and answered the phone.

'Hey.' Cameron's deep voice reverberated down the line and she swallowed hard, almost light-headed with longing for him. A huge smile broke out on her face even as she reminded herself that she didn't yet know his reason for calling.

'Hi,' she replied cautiously.

'I wasn't sure you'd even answer my call,' Cameron continued, sounding sheepish. 'You know, after the horrible things I said to you.'

Oh my God, he doesn't hate me! Intensely relieved, River's grin widened. 'I'm just glad to hear your voice! I've been really scared you meant it – about us breaking up, I mean.' She knew she was babbling but she was much too happy to care.

'Well, that's a relief. Not that you were scared, I mean, but... well, you know.'

She heard the smile in his voice and desperately wished he were close enough for her to grab him into the most enormous hug. She was grinning so hard that her cheeks hurt, and she forced herself to listen to the words gushing down the phone.

'Babe, I'm not happy you lied to me, but... I love you and I want us to work.'

'Me, too,' she burbled. Gone were her reservations about their relationship being in a rut. Now she could hear his lovely voice, all River wanted to do was fix things between them.

'I'm *so* sorry I didn't tell you the truth. I've felt sick about it, and nothing's been the same without you. Oh my God, Cam, I've missed you so *much!*'

'I've missed you, too,' he admitted. 'You were right, I *was* jealous about you and Donald Ayo. I was furious you lied to me, but it really tore me apart to see you sitting there all cosied up with him over a bottle of wine. I haven't heard a single good thing said about that man. He's a bully and a snake, and I wouldn't trust him an inch.'

'Well, you've got nothing to be jealous about.'

'Yeah, I know. But babe, I *need* to be able to trust you. If we're going to get past what happened, you've got to promise me there'll be no more lies. Can you agree to that?'

River groaned inwardly, but there was no escaping the question and she gave a mental shrug. If it took a vow of honesty to make things right again with Cameron, then she had no choice.

'Fine,' she sighed. Then conscious of how unenthused she sounded, she added hastily, 'I mean, yes, of course I promise. No more lies.'

'Good. So, now let's celebrate us getting back to normal again. It's still early and I can come and pick you up. How about we go over to Kwame's for drinks and something to eat? He's hired a new chef who makes the best kebabs. We can come back to mine afterwards and I'll show you how much I've missed you. I'll even tidy up this place just for you,' he teased.

River giggled and was about to agree when she remembered why she was sitting on a chair in her underwear. The designer dress and her waiting shoes seemed to mock her as she cast around the room, desperately seeking a way to avoid a fresh quarrel. Her instinctive reaction was to plead a headache, but then she remembered the promise she had made only moments earlier. *Why don't people understand that truth is not always a good thing?* With nothing else for it, River released the breath she hadn't realised she'd been holding into a regretful sigh. 'I'm so sorry. I'd love to see you, but I can't tonight.'

'Why not?' Cameron demanded, a note of suspicion entering his voice.

There really was no way around it. 'Because I'm going out with Donald Ayo.'

When he said nothing, River added hurriedly, 'Cam, it's not... look, it's a work thing. Well, it's a charity dinner, but he's promised to introduce me to people who could be new clients for Premier and...'

Feeling like she was digging a deeper hole for herself with every word she uttered, River bit her lip and waited for Cameron to say something. But he remained silent and after a long moment she tried again.

'Donald *knows* you and I are together. He felt bad that I was upset after... well, you know, that night at the restaurant. He could tell I was sad about us fighting and...' She tailed off miserably, and only then did Cameron interject.

'... and he thought he'd take advantage.'

'Cameron—'

'Just stop.' Suddenly he sounded utterly weary. 'I'm not going to keep doing this, so take your pick. Who do you want to be with? You need to decide if it's him or me.'

Despite feeling wretched about the turn the

conversation was taking, her boyfriend's command had River bristling. 'Don't issue ultimatums, Cameron. You know how much I hate that.'

'I said, him or me,' Cameron repeated doggedly. 'You need to decide right now.'

His uncompromising tone ignited a flash of anger which River tried to control. 'Please be *reasonable*! I've already said yes to Donald and I can't just let him down. His driver will be here at any minute.'

As if on cue, the doorbell sounded loudly, and River's eyes darted in frustration from the dress hanging on her wardrobe to the phone in her hand. Other than being unforgivably rude, there was nothing preventing her from changing her mind about going to the event with Donald. The property deal was done and dusted, and he no longer had a hold over her. Even the designer dress he had bought her, beautiful though it was, was not a gift she had sought.

But Cameron's high-handed attitude was making River increasingly resentful. What gave him the right to *demand* that she make a choice? Having ignored her calls for so long, he now expected her to simply drop her plans because *he'd* decided he was ready to make up. If Cameron really loved her, why did he never make the effort to see things from her point of view? Whatever Donald's faults, he had at least been kind enough to comfort her when she'd been upset and was even offering her an opportunity to turbocharge her career.

River heard her mother calling and she took a deep breath and tried to salvage the situation. 'Cameron, you're taking this entirely the wrong way. You asked me to be honest with you and that's exactly what I'm doing. I made a commitment, and I *want* to go. It's a prestigious event which I'd normally never be invited to and there'll be people there who buy property the way you and I buy clothes. Going to this fundraiser will open new doors for me and I would be crazy to turn it down.'

'Jesus, River! Is *everything* about money with you?'

She winced at the disgust she heard in his voice, and her own hardened. 'You know something? I'm sorry we're not all happy living hand to mouth and waiting around for our dreams to materialise. There's nothing wrong with having some ambition – not that *you* would know.'

The words slipped out before River could help herself. For a moment, the only sound she could hear was his ragged breathing and she fought back the tears forming behind her eyes. In the space of just a few minutes, her emotions had plummeted from the heights of exhilaration to the depths of despair.

'*Mama!* Where are you? The driver is waiting!' Her mother's high-pitched voice pierced through the bedroom door and River blinked back her unshed tears, silently pleading with Cameron to forgive her while the actual words remained stuck in her throat.

Then Cameron sighed deeply, and the sound stabbed through River's heart like a knife. 'We really *are* on different paths, aren't we?' he said sadly. 'I love you so much, but it's obvious I'm not the right man for you. You want someone who can open the kind of doors you're so desperate to walk through and we both need to stop making the other one feel bad for being who they are. Go to your millionaire and enjoy whatever he's promised you.'

After the briefest of pauses, he added quietly, 'Goodbye, River.'

This time, she was left in no doubt they were over.

Chapter 8

'Here, these are for you.'

River had been wrestling with a thick slab of steak on her plate and it took a moment for Donald's words to register. Looking up, she blinked rapidly as her eyes focused on a set of keys dangling from his finger. Grinning at the blank expression on her face, Donald placed the keys on the table and pushed them across the white tablecloth to the side of her plate.

River slowly put down her cutlery and reached for them, her gaze immediately drawn to a sparkling heart-shaped silver pendant attached to the keyring.

'What is this?' She frowned in puzzlement.

'Erm... keys? I imagine you've seen some before,' he laughed. 'To be specific, they're a set of keys to my new house... or rather to *our* new house. If you're interested, that is. I'll be moving in shortly and it could be the start of a new life for both of us.'

Stunned into silence, River absently stroked the pendant lying in the palm of her hand as she tried to come up with a response. Since their first kiss on the night of the charity dinner almost three months earlier, she had felt like a turbulent wave being swept along in a direction over which she had no control and by a force she couldn't withstand.

On that fateful evening, shocked by Cameron's

decision and numb with pain at the abrupt end to her five-year relationship, River had climbed into the back of the waiting chauffeur-driven car to meet Donald at the Conference Centre where she had forced a bright smile and posed alongside him on the red carpet. Despite being seated at a table with guests that included two famous actors, a rap star and a former Vice President, it had taken sheer willpower, aided by several glasses of wine, to play her part as Donald introduced her to a succession of people over the course of the evening. Reminding herself of what she had sacrificed for the opportunity, River had maintained her smile throughout the night while discreetly slipping one business card after another into her purse.

The smile had slipped when on their way out of the Conference Centre, Donald nodded in greeting at an attractive dark-skinned woman walking past them. 'That's Rachel de Sousa. She's a close friend of Nina's.'

River pulled a face but said nothing as Donald escorted her back to the waiting limousine, still singing Nina's praises. 'African art has really taken off on the international markets and Nina has sold me some beautiful pieces over the years which have proved to be good investments. If "Cameron ... boyfriend" has her for an agent, then he's in excellent hands.'

River swallowed the sudden lump constricting her throat and unable to help herself, blurted out huskily, 'More like "Cameron *ex*-boyfriend".'

Donald raised an eyebrow. 'So, he's definitely out of the picture?'

River reluctantly nodded and a flash of something

that looked like triumph crossed Donald's face. But before she could think about what she had seen, he stroked her cheek gently and tilted her face up to his. When his lips sought hers, River had returned Donald's kiss, far too miserable and angry with Cameron to care.

That kiss had opened the door to the whirlwind that was Donald Ayo, and before she knew it River found herself spending almost every free moment with him. Burying her pain at losing Cameron, she soon grew accustomed to joining Donald for dinner at expensive restaurants or accompanying him on champagne-fuelled outings with his crowd at his polo club. Initially feeling out of place, she quickly learned to move easily among the wealthy and well-connected people at the exclusive parties held in his celebrity friends' extravagant houses. Her client list was bulging, and Premier had acquired more properties on its books in the past quarter than over the entire year.

'Are you planning to give me an answer?' Donald's amused voice cut into her thoughts.

River sighed and dragged her mind back to her current predicament. Moving in with Donald was a huge leap from simply hanging out with him. Although she had always known that the expensive gifts he showered on her and the entrée he had facilitated into his high-spending clique would one day require some form of payback, he had accepted her clear wish to let their relationship develop at a pace she was comfortable with. Until now.

'I'm... flattered,' she said carefully. 'But this is a bit, well, unexpected. I thought we had agreed to take things slowly.'

He took a long swallow of beer. 'River, if we go any slower, we'll be going backwards. I haven't pressured you to take things further than you felt ready to, but it's been months now and frankly I don't see the point in beating around the bush. I've made it clear I want you and I've given you plenty of time to get to know me. It's time to take things to the next level and if we're living together, we'll have the privacy to do so without any interruptions or distractions.'

The intensity in his eyes made his meaning crystal clear, and River flushed and stared down at her half-eaten steak. The fact she lived at home and had been careful about visiting Donald's penthouse apartment had made it easier to make excuses and put him off whenever things grew too heated. But if she moved in with him, the time for excuses would be over.

After a moment, Donald shrugged. 'Look, maybe you don't love me yet, but you will in time. In any case, as you should know by now, being in love is overrated. Trust me, you're much better off without some romantic fantasy about men in your head and focusing instead on the benefits of our partnership. I told you the first time I met you that you're different. I could see immediately that you are very much like me – ambitious and ready to do whatever it takes to enjoy the good life.'

Cameron's parting words popped into River's mind along with a pang of sadness. Then Practical River reared her head to remind her she had wasted five years waiting while Cameron focused on his dreams. She was still short of her house fund target and if being with Donald would help her get what she wanted, why was she hesitating?

Cameron is your past and Donald can give you the future you want.

But then River remembered another obstacle, one she simply couldn't ignore. 'Donald, I can't just move in with you without us being... well, you know, official. My mother would literally go crazy if I so much as suggested it and even my dad, who doesn't involve himself in anything he doesn't have to, might have something to say.'

Looking supremely unconcerned, Donald took another sip of his drink and placed his glass on the table. 'You said right from the start that you aren't looking for marriage and let's be clear that neither am I. With that said, I can offer you the best of everything and your parents will come around when they see I can take care of you.'

Still troubled, River dropped the keys and picked up her fork, but her appetite had vanished. After watching her push vegetables around her plate for a few minutes, Donald shook his head in exasperation. 'I've been patient for months, River, but don't confuse me with Cameron. I'm not some sucker who's going to hang around forever waiting for you to decide whether you're in or out.'

He nodded towards the keyring on the table. 'Take those keys and go over to the house tomorrow. The interior designers have finished, and you can see what's been done to the place. And then I want you to make a decision.'

River slipped the keys into her bag without comment and forced down a few mouthfuls of food. Donald might think they had spent enough time together for her to know him, but the reality was she felt no closer now to fathoming the real man than she had at their first meeting. The image he allowed the outside world, including her, to see was of a highly successful and charming man with drive and confidence by the bucketload. While he could be domineering and occasionally high-handed, he was also unfailingly courteous to her and had been supremely generous. And yet, she still couldn't shake her instinct that beneath his urbane, sophisticated exterior lay someone far more unpredictable, ruthless, and – yes, dangerous. Someone who had no qualms about going after what he wanted, no matter the cost.

* * *

River walked into the house and closed the front door behind her. The sunlight streaming through the glass ceiling of the atrium bathed the hallway in a golden light that immediately lifted her spirits. She stood motionless, soaking in the atmosphere and letting the tranquil surroundings soothe her turbulent emotions. Then she took a deep breath and set about her task.

As River wandered through the silent rooms on the ground floor, it was clear that in the three months since Donald had signed the contract, the Marula Heights house had been transformed from a stunning house into an extraordinary showpiece by his carefully selected – and ridiculously expensive – interior designers. Standing in the doorway of the enormous dining room dominated by a mahogany table that could easily seat thirty people, she ran her fingers over the silky texture of the imported wallpaper before moving into the adjoining living room. Here, the designers had deftly incorporated the new owner's love of hi-tech gadgets with the clean lines of the house and overwhelmed by the sheer luxury of her surroundings, River perched on the edge of one of two huge white corner sofas she knew Donald had ordered from Italy.

A few minutes later she ran lightly up the stairs, eager to see the changes made to the bedrooms. Once again, she marvelled at the quality of the interior design and how each room had been given its own character with imaginative touches ranging from different colour palettes and artwork to carefully chosen bathroom accessories. It was clear no detail had been overlooked.

Standing in front of the final door on the landing, River's heart pounded a little faster when she reached for the handle. Although she was in the house with Donald's blessing, she still felt like an intruder as she pushed open the door and entered the master bedroom. The space felt more intimate despite the black and grey colour scheme and stark white walls. A huge abstract painting in bold shades of red and purple hung on the wall facing the bed and brought a lone splash of colour to the monochrome furnishings.

River's eyes wandered to the huge circular bed in the centre of the room and she felt a flush of heat rising from her chest. Donald wasn't due to move in for another week, but for a moment it felt like he was right there in the room with her. She sat down heavily on the edge of the bed and tried to bring her chaotic thoughts into some semblance of order. She had always known Donald's plan was to take up residence as soon as the decorators completed the final touches. What she hadn't counted on was his plan extending to her moving in with him. With a deep sigh, she lay back on the bed and surveyed the spotlight-studded ceiling while she reflected soberly on her options. Although she was flattered by Donald's attention, she also knew she wasn't in love with him. But then, as Practical River argued persuasively, what did love have to do with it? Living in an exclusive community like Marula Heights was more than River had ever imagined, and this gorgeous house was far grander than any of the properties pinned onto her vision board. Donald was clearly crazy about her and was offering her the chance to live in the kind of house she had always dreamed of. Wasn't this the lifestyle she had been scrimping and saving for? She could still continue putting aside money for her own property investments but maybe it was time to stop squirrelling away almost every penny she earned and, as Donald kept insisting, simply enjoy herself for a change?

Chapter 9

River jerked upright as the sound of her mobile ringtone carried through the open door into the master bedroom. She scrambled off the bed and raced downstairs to grab the handset she had left on the mahogany cabinet in the hallway.

'Hey girl! Where are you?'

'*Sly*!' she panted. 'Give me a second to catch my breath. I had to run to answer the phone.'

'Maybe you should spend more time at the gym and less time eating fancy dinners,' Sly scoffed. 'Where the hell are you? I haven't seen you for ages! What's going on?'

River drew in deep breaths to slow down her racing pulse and leaned against the cabinet, feeling horribly guilty. She had neglected her friends for weeks, and Sly most of all. Donald's referrals had swelled her client base so quickly that even Harvey who hated spending money unless he really had to had suggested she hire an assistant to help with the increased admin. Her social life now centred around Donald who insisted she accompany him to the seemingly endless round of social functions in his calendar.

'I'm at Donald's new house in Marula Heights. I was just about to leave—'

'Oh, that's so cool, wait there and I'll come over. I'm only about ten minutes away and I'm *dying* to see why you're so obsessed with the place. Text me the directions.'

'Sly, no—' River broke off, realising he had already ended the call. Donald wouldn't be pleased at her letting someone else into his private space. She was about to call Sly back when she reminded herself that he was her best and oldest friend, and instead she tapped out the address on her mobile. If Donald wanted her to move in with him, he would simply have to accept her friends.

Shortly afterwards, River heard the double toot of a car horn. She pressed the fob to open the gates and ran down the pathway to greet Sly, jumping on him the moment he emerged from his battered Toyota.

'Hi, stranger!' Sly grinned so widely his round eyes crinkled at the corners.

River hung onto his arm excitedly. 'Oh my God, I've missed you so much! I haven't seen you for almost *three* weeks! That's *so* crazy.'

Sly rolled his eyes. 'Well, what can I tell you? Whenever Mr *Start the Music* calls, the rest of us get tossed aside, it seems.' His expression changed as he turned towards the house and his eyebrows shot up. 'Wow, you weren't exaggerating!'

Dismissing Donald's certain disapproval, River tugged on her friend's arm. 'Come inside,' she urged. 'The designers have finished and it's absolutely stunning.'

Twenty minutes later, looking suitably stunned, Sly walked back to his car with River close beside him.

'Why do you have to go so soon?' she pouted. 'Can't we – I don't know, go and get a burger or a pizza or something?' She was thrilled to see Sly again and hated letting him go. Moreover, Donald was in meetings all day and the thought of spending her free Saturday on her own was not appealing. But instead of agreeing to her suggestion, Sly scrutinised his car keys in silence.

'What is it?' River asked suspiciously. 'And don't lie to me.'

'I beg your pardon! Unlike some people I know, I do *not* tell lies.'

'So then, spit it out.'

'We-ell,' Sly drawled, 'we can go and get something to eat if you want, but I'll have to go by the gallery first. I need to open up for a client to take measurements in the exhibition area.'

'Fine, so I'll wait while you do what you have to do. That's not a problem, is it?'

Sly shrugged. 'Not for me, but the client is Cameron and he's coming with his agent friend.'

'*Oh!*' River breathed, completely taken aback. She hadn't spoken to Cameron since the night of the charity dinner and she opened her mouth to suggest Sly went without her. Then she changed her mind and closed it again. Maybe seeing her ex-boyfriend would bring closure and allow her to move on with Donald, she mused. Or maybe, a little voice inside her said, you want to see him again and find out how he feels about you.

Sly looked troubled by her silence. 'I can meet you afterwards if you like?'

'No, no, it's fine. Cameron and I are bound to run into each other at some point in this town, so it might as well be now,' River said. She tried to sound breezy, even as little butterflies of nerves fluttered in the pit of her stomach.

'I'll just get my bag and lock up.'

Before Sly could comment, River hurried up the path towards the house, trying to bring her suddenly racing pulse back under control. Grabbing the new Fendi handbag Donald had bought her the previous week, she quickly locked the front door and within minutes she was back with Sly.

'Shall I ride with you?' she asked.

'If you want. I'll drop you back here later to pick up your car. Where is it, by the way?' He raised a hand to shade his eyes from the glare of the sun as he scanned the large compound.

'Over there,' River muttered, pointing to a white Mercedes convertible parked under the shade of an imposing acacia tree.

Sly's mouth dropped open and his eyes grew so wide she thought he was having a stroke. 'River, you have *got* to be kidding me! How in the *hell*—?'

'Calm down, it's not like I actually bought it! It's one of Donald's cars and he prefers me to drive it when I'm not working. According to him, having the Premier Properties logo on my car is tacky and driving a Mini doesn't impress anyone. Come on,' she added impatiently as she pulled open the door. 'Let's go or we – I mean, you'll be late.'

Chapter 10

River quietly nursed the butterflies in her stomach while Sly navigated the weekend traffic. She couldn't help her rising excitement at seeing Cameron again, even after the awful argument that had ended their relationship. Disregarding her supposed goal of seeking closure, her mind was instead racing furiously towards a different conclusion. Maybe Cameron would be reminded of all the good times when he saw her again, she ruminated. Perhaps he would even—

She flinched as Sly tapped her knee impatiently. 'Hey, lady, I'm talking to you!'

'Sorry, I was miles away.' She flashed him an apologetic smile. 'What did you say?'

'I asked how work is going? The last time I saw you – you remember, that day last month when you dumped me *again* because Donald wanted you to go somewhere with him? – you told me your client list had exploded.'

Ignoring the sarcasm, River nodded. 'I'm telling you, Sly, Donald has hooked me up with so many people and they are really serious about investing their money into property. They all hang out with each other and it's, like, as soon as one person says they're using us, everyone they know decides they should be doing the same. I've got another Marula Heights house on my books and I'm putting together virtual tours for a couple of new clients in Dubai. We've got people now just randomly dropping into the office and asking us to take over renting out their apartments for them. I got a call yesterday from – well, let's just say it's someone *very* high up in government who said I come highly recommended.'

Sly kept his eyes on the road as they approached the busy town centre. 'Well, I suppose it's nice that the millionaire is good for more than expensive meals. Harvey must be over the moon!'

River laughed. 'He can't believe the amount of business I've brought in. He's promised to hire an assistant so I can focus on servicing my clients and generating new business.' She tugged at the seat belt strapped across her lacy top and twisted round in her seat to face Sly. 'Donald says I should stop making Harvey money and set up my own real estate company. What do you think?'

Sly darted a shocked glance at her. 'But that's mad! You've worked with Harvey for years!'

'Yes, and I've worked my butt off for him. But if I were running my own business, I could keep all the commission from my sales and not just take a cut—' She broke off as Sly sucked his teeth loudly and shook his head.

'*What*?' she protested. 'I've always made it clear I'm ambitious. I have big dreams and I'm not embarrassed to admit that. Why are *you* so shocked, anyway? You hate your job.'

'I know, but I haven't left, have I?' Sly said quietly. 'There *is* such a thing as loyalty, River. My boss drives me mad, but do you know how much money Nelson donated towards my dad's funeral? And he didn't say a word to make me feel bad when I couldn't handle things at work for weeks after Pops died. Harvey has been there for you right from the beginning. Don't forget he was the one who gave you a chance when the other property companies turned you down.'

'Of *course*, I'm grateful for everything Harvey's done for me, but that doesn't mean I can't make progress with my life. Like Donald says, everything comes to an end eventually and we all move on at some point. It's nothing personal. Sometimes we just outgrow things.'

'And people too, from the sounds of it. Who are you outgrowing next? Me?'

River looked at him in horror. 'Don't be silly, you're my best friend!' She prudently decided not to share Donald's advice about investing her time only in friends who could take her places and quickly changed the subject.

'Sly, I need your advice on the best way to break the news to my mother that I'm considering moving in with Donald. He's asked me and I'm thinking of saying yes but you know what Ma is like.'

Sly swerved out of his lane in shock, inciting angry toots from an approaching vehicle. 'Are you kidding me? You're actually planning to *marry* the man?'

'No, of course not,' she said in exasperation. 'I don't care about getting married, but you know how Ma insists on things being done "properly"' – she crooked her fingers into air quotes – 'and all that. She used to go on at me to dump Cameron but now I'm seeing someone successful, I bet she'll still find something to complain about. Don't look at me like I'm crazy. If you think about it, Donald and I have been practically inseparable for months. Now his house is ready, he thinks we should take things to the next level. You've seen the place, isn't it *amazing*?'

Sly broke in impatiently. 'River, what exactly is this about? Do you love Daddy Donald or his mansion? Which is it? Because to be honest – and you *know* I'm all about being honest – the only thing I'm hearing you get excited about is his house!'

'That's not true,' she denied, affronted by the idea she would move in with a man simply because of where he planned to live. Admittedly, she did love Donald's house, but what was wrong with that? *Anyone* would kill to live in Marula Heights.

'Okay, so name one person who would say no to moving into a mansion on that estate?' she challenged.

'It depends on what they have to give up,' was Sly's acid response. 'Listen, I'm not judging you – well, not much anyway. All I'm saying is if that's what you want, fine, but at least be honest about it. Let's face it, you're a free agent now Cameron's out of the picture.'

He spotted River's involuntary wince and chuckled wickedly. 'Oh, I'm sorry, is it too soon? Don't worry, you'll get over it. From what I'm hearing, it looks like he has. He's out constantly with that new agent of his. Jacob Nartey saw them at the Vogue club last week looking very comfortable.'

River snorted in irritation. '*Puh-lease*! Jacob's lying – Cam hates clubbing.'

'Not anymore, it would seem. Anyhow, don't change the subject. Why are you even considering moving in with Donald? You've been stashing money away for the longest time to buy your own place.'

River was saved from answering as Sly turned into the gallery car park and pulled up a few parking bays away from a sleek blue Mazda with tinted windows. She instinctively knew Cameron was in the car and she struggled to breathe as her butterflies returned in full force.

'You go ahead and do what you need to do,' she said, her voice suddenly shaky with nerves. 'I'll wait here for you.' Now that she was within a few metres of encountering her ex, she badly needed more time to compose herself.

Sly left the car without argument and walked over to where Cameron and Nina were emerging from the Mazda. Thankful that the huge Range Rover parked next to Sly's car prevented her from being seen, River craned her neck to peer through her window, watching as the two men shook hands and Cameron introduced Nina. After a brief exchange, Sly led them down the pathway that ran alongside the building to the main entrance, and the moment they were out of sight, River collapsed against the seat cushions in relief. Even the brief glimpse she'd caught of Cameron had left her weak with longing for him, and she groaned aloud in sheer frustration. Coming here had been a bad idea; instead of bringing closure, she was now aching to throw herself into her ex's arms and pretend the last three months had never happened.

***

Almost thirty minutes spent in a roasting hot car overruled River's reluctance to reveal herself. Her face was damp from the heat while the intense humidity was playing havoc with her hair. Sly had walked off with the keys, rendering the air conditioning useless. Even with her door thrown wide open, the car still felt like an oven.

After waiting it out for a couple more minutes, River had had enough. Glancing around to check the coast was clear, she darted across the parking lot to stand under the shade of a large tree. She closed her eyes in relief and fanned herself with the newspaper she had grabbed from the back seat of Sly's car. As the gentle breeze cooled her heated skin, she relaxed and inhaled the sweet scents wafting down from the branches of the flowering tree.

The sound of a quiet cough cut through her dreamy state and she opened her eyes to find herself face to face with Cameron, Nina and Sly. She stared dumbly at them until Sly quickly turned to Nina with a barrage of questions, all the while steering her away towards the Mazda and leaving Cameron and River alone under the tree.

Cameron glanced across to where Sly's Toyota was parked with its passenger door wide open, and turned back to River with an incredulous expression. 'Have you been sitting out in this heat all the time we were in the gallery? Why didn't you just say hello when you got here and come inside?'

River's tongue was glued to the roof of her mouth as she tried to find a plausible alternative to the truth that risking sunstroke was preferable to facing an ex-boyfriend you couldn't stop thinking about. Cameron looked so handsome with his close-cropped hair emphasising his sculpted jawline that she had to hold her arms firmly to her sides to avoid reaching for him and embarrassing them both. Unlike the Cameron of old, there wasn't a speck of paint visible on his dark blue denims and his pale blue linen shirt looked crisp and new. She looked over at Sly who was deliberately blocking Nina's view of River and Cameron and smiled faintly. Despite her friend's efforts to give her some privacy, Cameron's stern expression was hardly encouraging.

The silence was becoming unbearable, and in desperation River blurted out the first thing that popped into her head. 'Sooo... you're really putting on an exhibition, then?'

Cameron gave her a sidelong look and then said dryly, 'Yeah, Nina's working on a virtual and in-person exhibition which sounds crazy to me, but she knows what she's doing. I'm just grateful she believes in me and my work.'

'I'm very happy for you,' River offered, keeping her tone as conciliatory as she could. It felt absurd to be having such a stilted exchange with a man she had loved for years and completely inconceivable that her once affectionate boyfriend had been transformed into this incredibly hot stranger with cold eyes.

'So, how are you getting on, River?' He sounded very like someone being forced to make polite conversation. 'You and Donald Ayo seem to be quite the couple now. I saw a picture of you in the papers the other day looking very loved up at some charity thing.'

On the verge of admitting the truth, River stopped herself, inexplicably hurt by Cameron's matter-of-fact tone and his clear indifference to her being with another man. Why had she imagined he might have a change of heart when he saw her, she wondered? Sly was right, and Cam was clearly over her and now playing happy couples with Nina.

'I'm doing great.' She gave a brittle laugh that sounded unnatural even to her own ears. 'Business is booming and all that.'

'That's good news, isn't it? Looks like you've got everything you wanted, so I'm glad you're happy.'

'Of course, I am. Things couldn't be better.' River couldn't have sounded breezier if she'd tried, and she flushed as Cameron's short laugh mocked her attempt at nonchalance.

'I see you're still lying to me, River. Or maybe this time it's just to yourself.'

The pity in his eyes made her toes curl with mortification but before she could reply, Nina walked over and hooked her arm into Cameron's. Seemingly oblivious to any tension in the air, she grinned cheerfully at River.

'You look familiar. We've met before, haven't we?' She screwed up her nose and then exclaimed, 'You were at The Embassy with Donald Ayo... yes, I remember now. You have an unusual name... *River*! That's it.'

She looked up at Cameron curiously. 'I didn't realise you two knew each other.'

For the briefest of moments Cameron hesitated, and then he shrugged lightly. 'I thought I did, but I was mistaken. Shall we go?' With a curt nod at River, he draped an arm around Nina's shoulders and guided her back to the car.

Chapter 11

'Mama! Listen to me well. There is no way I will permit you to live with a man without benefit of – well, *anything*! What is he saying? No knocking, no drinks, no engagement? *Haba!* Why do my daughters want to see me in my grave?'

Torn between anger and laughter as she watched her mother pace up and down the crowded living room, River was sorely regretting having instigated the drama now in full flow. Still smarting from her encounter with Cameron the day before and determined to show she could also move on, River had chosen what had, up to that point, been a quiet Sunday afternoon to broach the subject of Donald's proposal to her mother. Appalled at her daughter's desire to live with a man she had known for only a matter of months, her mother had immediately called a family conference. Within the space of an hour, River's three aunties had been ushered into the living room and Sefa had raced home from Kojo's house in response to her sister's urgent plea for back-up. River's father, comfortably ensconced in his favourite armchair, had been barred by his wife from even touching his newspaper until their daughter agreed not to shame her family by cohabiting with a man who, despite his wealth, appeared strangely unwilling to do the right thing.

River sighed and shook her head. 'Honestly, Ma, are

you ever happy? You hated Cameron because he didn't have a full-time job and now you've got a problem with Donald who's only trying to take care of me and give me a good life.'

Her mother stopped her pacing to glare at her daughter. 'Mama, I don't *hate* anyone. How can you say such a thing to a good Christian woman? Have you ever known me to miss Church? That boy comes from a decent family, so how can I hate him? No, my only problem was that he wasn't prepared to take a professional job and earn a decent salary to provide for my daughter.'

Shrugging off her mother's talent for rewriting history, River appealed directly to her audience. 'Aunties, please… can you tell my mother I'm thirty years old and a grown woman who earns her own living. I don't need her permission if I choose to live with someone!'

River's aunties were huddled together on a sofa observing the verbal battle between mother and daughter, and they immediately exchanged uneasy glances.

'My daughter, this is not an easy request,' Auntie Essie began tentatively. 'Yes, you are an adult but…' she faltered and turned to her sister who was wedged in beside her. Having left her house in a hurry, Auntie Mansa had arrived in her house slippers and with her wig askew.

'Essie is right. This is a very delicate situation,' Auntie Mansa entreated. 'My dear, I think it is best if this man presents himself to us. That way, we can judge for ourselves if he is sincere in his intentions.'

River's mother nodded in agreement. 'You make a good point, Mansa. What kind of man invites an innocent young girl to live with him even before he has met the mother – or the father,' she added belatedly with a glance over at her husband.

'River is hardly an innocent young girl,' Sefa murmured in amusement from the armchair in which she had been watching the proceedings. 'I'm sorry, Ma, but I think you're getting this way out of proportion. River's a big girl and she can make her own decisions.'

'*Thank* you, Sef,' River flashed her sister an appreciative smile and then turned back to her mother. 'Okay, so if I get Donald to come and meet you and Dad, will you at least be polite and hear him out? I don't want to embarrass myself by making him come over here if you're going to go all traditional and insist on marriage.'

Auntie Essie sighed deeply. 'Marriage is a blessing, but only if it is to the right man.' There was a deferential hush for a moment. Auntie Essie's husband had been missing in action for over a decade, having initially left for the Middle East on a six-month project. His sporadic visits home had eventually ceased, and it had been years since anyone in the family had seen him.

Auntie Frema's deep voice broke the awkward silence. 'Marriage may not be a perfect institution and as you say, you are now an adult. But remember that if you give a man all the benefits of marriage without the responsibility, well...,' she tailed off with a shrug.

Sefa had been scrolling through her phone and she looked up with a grin. 'Ma, there's an article on the City Gossip website about Donald Ayo. I'll send you the link and you can read up about him before you meet.' She tapped her phone again and her expression changed.

'Erm, sis, have you seen this picture of Cameron?'

River felt her stomach muscles tense. 'What picture?'

She winced as Sefa held up her phone to show a close-up of Cameron and Nina. They were looking deeply into each other's eyes and laughing, both clearly oblivious to the photographer.

'Is that Cameron's new girlfriend?' Auntie Essie asked curiously, her eyes darting between the picture and River's set expression.

Sefa scrolled further down the screen. 'It looks like it, Auntie. It says here, "Up and coming artist Cameron King is the latest buzz in the City. As the handsome breakout star prepares for his inaugural exhibition in Accra's biggest gallery, word on the street is that King and his sexy agent, Nina Arthur, are developing a very special partnership. City Gossip wonders: are these two more than friends?"'

'Thanks, Sef. Just rub my face in it, why don't you?' River scowled.

'You're the one who wants to move in with another man. What do you care what Cameron's up to?'

What indeed? River returned her focus to bringing the family meeting to a speedy conclusion. 'Ma, like I was saying, if I can get Donald to come and introduce himself to you, will you promise not to give him the third degree about marriage?'

'Don't be rude, Mama!' her mother exclaimed indignantly before turning her ire on her husband. '*Kofi!* why are you sitting there in silence as if I am the only one here with a daughter. Please talk to your child!'

River's father leaned back in his chair and gazed at his older daughter in silence and she could have sworn she saw his lips twitch. Then he scratched his chin thoughtfully and turned to his wife.

'My dear, let's deal with this matter calmly. I certainly insist on meeting the man who wants to spirit my daughter away from me, but we must also recognise that River is an independent woman who will make her own choices.'

River grinned triumphantly, but before she could speak her father held up his hand and his voice took on a serious tone. 'River will also make her own mistakes, and I believe she will learn from both.'

* * *

After a long morning showing a prestigious but particularly fussy client around a property, River was back at Premier Properties and making her way to her desk when Harvey stuck his head outside his office door and beckoned her over. Stopping only to deposit her handbag on her chair, she made a beeline for her boss's office, a spacious glass-panelled room with blinds he left permanently open to keep an eye on his staff.

'You just missed your boyfriend,' Harvey muttered as she walked in and closed the door behind her.

'Really?' River asked, baffled. Even when he had been negotiating the Marula Heights property with Harvey, Donald had never set foot in their office. She also specifically remembered telling him she had a client meeting that morning.

'Did he say what he wanted or leave a message?'

'Not exactly.' Harvey replied brusquely. He looked so disgruntled that for a moment River wondered if he had been treating himself to dodgy street food again.

'Is there something you want to tell me?' Harvey's normally genial expression was scrunched into a deep scowl.

River frowned in puzzlement. 'I'm sorry, but I don't know what you mean.'

He leaned back in his chair and cleared his throat. 'Look, it's up to you if you're thinking of leaving Premier, but I would have hoped you would at least tell me yourself.'

'*Leaving*! But why—?'

'I mean, after all these years we've worked together, why wouldn't you at least—?'

'Harvey, I don't have any plans to leave!'

He looked at her doubtfully. 'Are you sure? Donald sounded quite certain.'

'*Donald*? Okay, hold on a minute. Harvey, please, what *exactly* did he say to you?'

'Well, he came here asking for you and I told him you were showing a house in Kanda. Instead of leaving, he seemed to want to chat, which I have to say I found quite strange. I don't think the man has exchanged even one word with me since he bought his mansion.'

River struggled to curb her impatience as she waited for her boss to get to the point. Harvey narrated his stories in the most long-winded way possible and any attempts to speed up his delivery only made things worse.

'... then he asked me how you were getting on. I told him you are doing a brilliant job – which of course you are. Then, straightaway, he said you're an excellent salesperson and he was sure I would miss you very much now you're leaving to start your own business.'

Dismayed by the hurt in Harvey's voice, River cursed herself for ever going along with Donald's suggestion of setting up her own business. She had since made it plain to him that leaving her boss was not an option she was prepared to consider, so why had he told Harvey the exact opposite?

'He had *no* right to say that to you! Honestly, Harvey, Donald is the one who keeps harping on about me setting up on my own. I won't lie, I did briefly consider it. But I wouldn't do that to you. I promise.'

Much to her relief, Harvey's face cleared. 'Well, I don't know what's wrong with that Ayo man or why he lied to me but I'm very pleased to hear your assurances, River.' His heavy features broke into a smile. 'You're an important part of the Premier family and it wouldn't be the same here without you. Of course, if one day you decide to set up your own company, I will give you my blessing – but not my clients. Now then, tell me how the viewing went this morning. Is the Minister likely to make an offer?'

Chapter 12

Suppressing a yawn, River pulled out her make-up bag and flopped onto the chair in front of her dressing table. For the first time since Donald had swept her into his celebrity-filled world, she would happily have swapped tonight's glitzy event for a quiet evening at home watching a video with Sefa.

She dotted concealer under her eyes to mask the dark shadows before applying a thick layer of foundation. Peering into the mirror, she sighed at the prospect of another evening putting on a show of bubbliness in front of the same groups of designer-clad women and faking interest in conversations which never strayed far from the latest fashions and the best beauty treatments. The men weren't much better, River thought moodily, touching up her brows with light, feathery strokes. All they did was down copious glasses of expensive brandy and argue about politics – when they weren't pretending to talk to her about property while attempting a surreptitious feel of her bottom. It hadn't taken her long to recognise the type who slipped her his business card in the hope of arranging a more personal type of viewing.

As she smoothed creamy eyeshadow onto her lids, River's mind flew back to the conversation with Harvey earlier that day. *What exactly was Donald playing at*? She had been pleasantly surprised by his reaction when she had broken the news that her family insisted on meeting him before there was any question of her living with him. He hadn't appeared unduly concerned, assuring her he could see their point and would arrange a meeting as soon as it was practicable.

If Donald was willing to make her happy by accepting her mother's conditions, River wondered, why was he then deliberately ignoring her expressed wish to stay in her job? Her initial excitement at the prospect of running her own company had quickly waned after further investigation had revealed the legal formalities, licences and costs involved. More importantly, despite her comments to Sly, she also hated the idea of abandoning Harvey and taking business from him when the property market was so volatile. She had explained all this to Donald at dinner the other evening and by going to her office when he knew she wouldn't be there to deliberately feed Harvey misinformation, he was obviously still bent on engineering her exit from Premier.

Picking up her hair brush, River pulled her thick curls into the smooth, tight chignon Donald favoured, securing the roll of hair with a handful of hairpins that dug into her scalp. At this rate, she would have a raging headache before the night was over, she thought gloomily, longing for the freedom of her loose natural curls. She slicked a layer of tinted gloss on her lips and then paused to scrutinise her face in the mirror. Her large dark eyes stared back at her and she scoured their depths for the sparkle that had once been there. For no apparent reason, Cameron's face came to mind and she felt her eyes well up. She blinked rapidly, hating herself for the direction her thoughts were taking. I'm just tired, she told herself, and pushed away from the dressing table.

With her hair and make-up done, River stepped into the dress laid out on her bed, slipped on her high heels, and then turned to check the fit in her full-length bedroom mirror. Just like the other designer gowns hanging in her wardrobe, the dress had arrived by courier earlier that day, and the silky royal blue design dipped low at the back and clung to her tiny waist before flaring out into a bell-shaped skirt that grazed her knees. She twisted back and forth and nodded approvingly. Donald might be a touch controlling and enjoy treating her like a dress-up doll just a little too much, but he had excellent taste in clothes.

* * *

'River, is that you?'

At the sound of her father's voice, River dropped the car keys she had picked up back onto the hall table. Dressed and ready to leave, she nonetheless turned away from the front door and retraced her footsteps across the hallway to the study. Entry to the room dubbed 'Dad's sanctuary' by his daughters was strictly by invitation, and River knocked gently on the half-open door and waited for his reply before walking in.

The study was lined with bookcases and sparsely furnished with a couple of filing cabinets, an old-fashioned desk and two cushioned armchairs. Her father was seated in one of the armchairs with a book open on his lap and the soft strains of classical music coming from a large old-fashioned CD player perched on a filing cabinet lent the room a calmness and serenity which were sorely lacking in the rest of the house.

'Hi, Dad,' River smiled affectionately at her father and he gestured for her to take a seat in the adjoining armchair.

'You look very nice,' he observed. 'You also look tired. It's only Wednesday and yet this is the third night you've been out this week.'

Surprised he had even noticed her comings and goings, River shrugged defensively. 'Donald sits on the boards of loads of organisations and charities and there's always some function or another he has to attend. He likes me going with him and it's also good for business if I network with these people.'

Her father looked pensive. 'I'm sure that's the case, although I wonder how many of the women at these social events are also juggling demanding full-time jobs?'

River grimaced but she couldn't deny the truth of her father's words. She'd be lucky if she got back home before two in the morning and would then have to be up again at six to get ready for work. The wives and girlfriends of Donald's wealthy friends had an army of domestic staff and most of them wouldn't dream of showing their faces before ten in the morning.

'I know, Dad, but it won't be like this forever. Right now, I have to stay focused and use this time to build my career so I can achieve my goals.'

Her father closed the book on his lap and placed it on the small table sandwiched between the two armchairs while River wondered why he had chosen this time to initiate a father-daughter talk. Tonight's event was scheduled to start in an hour but there was no way of escaping the conversation her father clearly intended to have.

'I'm worried about you, River.' He looked directly at her and a warm flush crept up into her cheeks.

'I'm absolutely fine, Daddy.' She hung her head, looking as guilty as a naughty five-year-old caught in a fib.

'I hear you moving around the house at all times of the night, which tells me you are not sleeping well. What is going on? First you inform us you are no longer involved with a man you have loved for, what, five years? Then you suddenly announce your wish to live with a man who is more than ten years your senior and who you have not even introduced to us.'

Put like that, it didn't exactly sound good, River conceded. 'Dad, I know it looks a bit rushed, but I honestly know what I'm doing. And Donald is really looking forward to meeting you and Ma,' she added, even though Donald had yet to suggest a date.

'All your mother and I want is for you to be happy, my dear. You have always been a hard worker, but looking at you now, I don't see the same happy, lively, young woman I know.'

River stared at the pointed tips of her silver high-heeled slingbacks and blinked back the unexpected tears in her eyes. 'I'm sorry if I've disappointed you, Dad. I'm just trying to live my life and be a success so you can be proud of me.'

After a moment of silence, she looked up and saw a tiny smile lighten the gravity of his expression.

'What's funny, Dad? I thought you were upset with me.'

'Do you know why I named you River?'

Bewildered by the change of subject, she nonetheless repeated the story she had heard so often. 'Because my eyes reminded you of the river in your hometown.'

'Yes, indeed. But there was another reason,' he said pensively. 'A river is a powerful force of nature and even as a tiny baby you gripped my fingers with such fierce strength that I knew you would be a fighter. I wanted to give you a name to remind you of your uniqueness and the power inside you to achieve great things. That interesting collage on your bedroom wall proves you have big aspirations.'

Slightly disconcerted to know her father had seen her vision board, River leaned forward in her seat. 'Dad, it's *because* I have great aspirations that I'm working such crazy hours.'

The music playing in the background faded into silence and her father studied her intently. 'My daughter, a river can be a force for good. Our river irrigated the land so farmers could cultivate fields that fed not only those of us in my hometown, but also the people in the surrounding countryside. But you need to remember that a river can also be destructive. It has the power to crash through dams and flood plains, killing the same crops and people it once nourished. So, my River, be careful. Because along with the strength to do great things comes the power to hurt others – as well as yourself. I want you to experience real love and sometimes that kind of love will call for sacrifices.'

River digested her father's words in silence. While he rarely voiced his opinions, his observations when he did speak were always shrewd and impossible to ignore.

'I know everyone thinks I behaved badly towards Cameron, but I really didn't mean to hurt him,' she said haltingly. 'I just didn't want to give up on everything I've been working towards.' Having started on the subject, her words gushed out. 'I felt so taken for granted, Dad, and he wasn't prepared to make any changes to make me happy. He gave me an ultimatum, which he knows I hate, and – well… I had to stand up for myself.'

'It's not for me to tell you what to do, my child, but don't mistake stubbornness for strength.'

With that, her father leaned back in his chair and picked up his book. 'I've kept you long enough and I don't want to make you late.'

River glanced at her watch and sprang to her feet. She was seriously late, and Donald with his fetish for punctuality was not going to be pleased.

'Good night, Dad.' She stooped to kiss her father and briefly pressed her cheek against his. She turned back when she reached the door and smiled at him fondly. 'You really *are* a dark horse. I can't believe you've actually seen my vision board.'

His eyes twinkled with mischief as he smiled and flipped the book open. 'Good night, my dear. Enjoy your evening.'

Chapter 13

As River stepped out of her Mini Cooper, the security guard closed the gate with a loud clang and crunched his way over the gravel towards her.

'Please, Madam, you can go inside. Boss is expecting you.'

River slipped her car keys into her bag and looked up at the imposing town house. Even from her vantage point of the driveway, River knew this was a special property. Three storeys high, it sat in half an acre of well-tended lawn embraced by bushes in full colourful bloom. She made her way up to the house, admiring the lush garden and beautifully manicured grass. As she approached the front door, it swung open and a stocky, middle-aged man stepped out on to the porch. Jerry Andoh was the wealthy owner of the town house and an acquaintance of Donald's. Not that he looked like much of a millionaire in his baggy shorts and white polo shirt that hugged his generous pot belly, River thought in amusement. His smile, however, was as genial as she remembered from their first meeting.

'Good morning, Mr Andoh. It's lovely to see you again.' She shook the hand he extended, and he clasped hers briefly between both of his own.

'The pleasure is all mine. I was waiting for you downstairs and I heard the gate. Please come in.'

He gestured to her to take the lead and then followed her inside. The hallway was wide and bright, and immediately to her right was a spacious open-plan formal living room. The door to her left, which River guessed led to the dining room, was closed.

'So, as I said on the phone, Miss Osei—'

'Please, call me River,' she interrupted.

He nodded in acknowledgement. 'River, I really need your advice. I bought this house a few years ago and at the time my wife was very insistent that town houses like these were the "in" thing. Unfortunately, these days my knees are not as strong as they once were and going up and down these stairs is a struggle. I've built a house out in Aburi which is single storey and will suit me much better and finally persuaded my wife we should sell this property. I've done my research since Donald suggested your company and I've heard very good things about you. So, now you know my situation, please tell me how you can help.'

Mr Andoh's smile was so infectious that River couldn't help smiling back. 'Can I just say that this is a beautiful house and I'm sure we won't have any problems with selling it.'

She flipped back the cover of her iPad and tapped open the checklist she used for her initial viewings. 'What I'll do today is have a good look around the property and take pictures and measurements so I can get to work on preparing a prospectus. I'll need to sign you up formally as a client before we start the process and I'll have our engagement contract sent to you tomorrow. After that, I can arrange an appointment for a valuation and then, with your approval, we'll start marketing and showing the house.'

Mr Andoh rubbed his hands with satisfaction. 'Excellent! In that case, let's get started. My wife had an appointment at the beauty salon, but she should be here shortly.'

His weak knees didn't slow him down as he marched her through the ground floor rooms. Given the chance, River would have lingered to admire the high ceilings and generously proportioned spaces, but instead she quickly noted the room dimensions and snapped a series of shots for the sales brochure. The Andohs' taste in furniture veered towards the dark and old-fashioned, and the room she had correctly guessed to be the dining room was dominated by a huge dining table with chairs upholstered in a dated brocade. She could only hope prospective buyers would see beyond the décor, and fortunately, the kitchen was huge and fitted with modern appliances.

River was measuring the cosily furnished family room on the first floor when they heard through the open louvre windows the toot of a car horn followed by the sound of clanging metal.

'That must be my wife.' Mr Andoh levered himself out of the sofa he had collapsed into and headed towards the landing. 'I'll let her know we're upstairs.'

River concentrated on taking pictures from different angles of the room and she was scrolling through the shots to check the quality when she heard a familiar laugh. Startled, she looked up to see Mr Andoh ushering Donald into the room.

'What are *you* doing here?' she blurted out, too shocked to remember her manners.

Donald raised an eyebrow and then said smoothly, 'I was in the area, so I decided to drop in and see Jerry.'

Looking slightly bemused, Mr Andoh nodded. 'Well, young River here is doing an excellent job and I'm very pleased you introduced us. Now, what can I offer you?'

'I wouldn't say no to some coffee if it's not too much trouble.'

River watched in disbelief as Donald patted her new client jovially on the shoulder as if her business meeting had suddenly become a social visit. Donald had been present when she had arranged this morning's appointment with Jerry Andoh so why pretend he was here on some random and impulsive whim? Where she wouldn't have dreamed of interrupting *his* work, what gave him the right to saunter into hers? Whatever Donald's game, it was becoming increasingly disturbing and she wasn't prepared to play.

'I need to view the bedrooms on the top floor, so why don't I leave you two to chat while I finish up?' Before Donald could object, she left them and raced up the spiral staircase racking her brains and trying to understand why Donald was checking up on her. His behaviour had been growing increasingly more proprietary in recent weeks with frequent phone calls throughout the day and random text messages, particularly on the rare evenings he didn't insist on her company. But today was the first time he had physically intruded on her work, and the notion that a high-profile tycoon with business interests that easily filled his working day had driven across town to see what she was doing left River feeling chilled rather than flattered.

It had been a month since Donald had moved into his Marula Heights mansion and he had yet to broach the subject of meeting her parents. Secretly welcoming the breathing space, River was making no effort to urge him to do so despite her mother's impatient queries. While Donald remained a stranger to her parents, she could maintain her position that moving in with him was out of the question.

The sound of the men's laughter travelled up from the lower floor as River worked her way through the four large bedrooms, taking measurements and photographs as speedily as she could manage. As much as she welcomed the opportunity to sell Jerry Andoh's massive town house, she suddenly couldn't wait to get out of there.

* * *

'What do you mean he just showed up?' Even through the phone, Sly sounded appalled.

River pulled herself up into a sitting position on her bed and crossed her legs. Although she felt faintly disloyal for spilling the beans about Donald's intrusion into her client meeting, she was desperate for another opinion on the strange behaviour of the man with whom she was on the verge of entering a committed relationship. This was one time when she needed complete honesty and there was no one better than Sly to tell her the truth.

She put the phone on speaker mode and balanced the handset on her knee. 'It was so weird. One minute I was taking down room measurements and then suddenly the man is standing there with some crazy story about how he just happened to be in the area. First of all, it was the middle of a working day and secondly, since when is Trasacco anywhere near his office at Airport?'

Sly was silent for a moment. 'Maybe he's paranoid about you sleeping with someone else now you and he are – well, you know.'

River sighed inwardly and weighed up the risk of confessing. She already had more than enough drama to contend with. But she needed Sly's advice too badly to skimp on the truth and so she said baldly, 'We're not.'

'Not what?'

'Not sleeping together. I mean, obviously we kiss and stuff, but—'

'Are you *serious*? After all this time? What the actual—?' The incredulity in his voice spilled through the phone speaker into the bedroom. Then, just as she had known he would, Sly launched into a bitter rant about her disrespecting their friendship by withholding crucial facts about her relationship. When he eventually calmed down enough for River to apologise, it was clear her revelation had served only to deepen Sly's misgivings.

'So, the man doesn't want to sleep with you, but he does want to control you and make sure no one else, including his happily married friend, gets too close? That's *messed up*, River! Come on, you've got to admit his behaviour is weird. What the hell is wrong with you?'

'I don't know. I just thought he was being a gentleman and respecting my wishes by not pushing me...' She ground to a halt, feeling foolish. Donald Ayo was an attractive, wealthy, and highly sought-after man who for months had plied her with expensive clothes and the use of a luxury car, not to mention business contacts and an invitation to move into his mansion. Even to her own ears, her justification for why he wasn't pressing her to sleep with him sounded ridiculous. Donald had made it abundantly clear from the outset he was attracted to her and indeed there had been many times he would kiss her passionately, but then pull back. River, who was still unsure if she cared enough to encourage him to go further, hadn't troubled herself to wonder why Donald wasn't pushing for more.

'Well, if it's not sex that he's after, then it's power,' Sly cautioned. 'Either way you need to be careful. Guys like that are used to being in charge and the way he turned up without any warning sounds to me like he's trying to show you he's the boss. I mean, look at what he did to poor Harvey!'

River chewed on her lip, pondering over Donald's brazen attempt to sabotage her job. 'D'you know he wasn't the slightest bit embarrassed or apologetic when I accused him of lying to Harvey. He just shrugged and said he was trying to encourage me not to limit my horizons by staying at Premier. It's like he wasn't listening to a word I said, because the next minute he offered to hire me a small office so I can work for myself.'

'By yourself, you mean,' Sly said darkly.

River frowned. 'What are talking about?'

'Oh my God, sis! Can you seriously not you see what this guy is doing? I've read about men like him. They try and isolate you from your friends and make you totally dependent on them.'

'Sly, *puh-lease*! I live in a house with an army of family members. How exactly is he going to isolate me?' she scoffed.

'Well, he managed to get you away from Cameron, didn't he?'

'That wasn't Donald's fault. Cam was the one being stubborn and refusing to understand—'

'Why you were going out with another man – i.e. the very same Donald,' Sly cut in. 'You keep saying Cameron was being unreasonable, but can you honestly blame him? How would *you* have felt if it were the other way round?'

River flushed, recalling how the simple act of Nina taking Cameron's arm had unleashed a savage urge to slap the woman.

'Whatever,' River said dismissively. Thinking about Cameron was too distracting and much too painful. She straightened her legs and lay back against the pillows, trying to bring the conversation back on track.

'I honestly think you're being a bit overdramatic about this. I totally agree Donald is used to getting his own way and, while it's annoying, I don't believe there's anything sinister about his motives.'

Sly's voice was loaded with scepticism. 'Are you sure about that? Okay then, tell me the last time you hung out with me without looking at your watch every ten minutes and running off to meet Donald the second he called? And before you make up some rubbish excuse, it's not just me – what about your other friends? Aku was asking after you the other day and she said none of the girls see you anymore.'

'That's because I've been *busy*!' River exploded in exasperation. 'I'm working crazy hours for my clients, and Donald's social calendar is permanently full! Don't any of you understand how stressed I am? I'd love to hang out but I'm under a lot of pressure right now. Sly, I'm begging you, please don't turn into my mother. She's wanted me to find a man who earns good money for years, and now she keeps having a go at me and telling me I've changed.'

'She's right,' Sly agreed bluntly. 'I've never judged you for wanting to be a tycoon before you turn forty, but at this rate, you'll end up a very rich forty-year-old with no friends. You wanted my honest opinion, so I'm telling you. I'm not seeing the same River I've known for ever, and you need to be on your guard with this Donald Ayo. We both know his reputation and even though he's coming across all cool and sophisticated, there's something shady about him. You know what they say about still waters running deep.'

A little later as she prepared for bed, River thought again about Sly's words and rubbed the sudden goose bumps on her bare arms. Sly was just being dramatic as usual, she reassured herself, switching off her bedside light and snuggling deep beneath her bedcovers. But as she drifted into sleep, a little voice niggled at the edge of her consciousness. *Sly never lies.*

Chapter 14

Donald wiped his lips with a white linen napkin and nodded his thanks as Monica, the housekeeper he had hired soon after moving into the mansion, cleared away the breakfast dishes. River reluctantly handed over her own empty plate, greedily eyeing the crumbs from the delicious croissants she had just consumed. If she had been on her own, she would have dabbed up each last flake of buttery pastry and toasted almond. The fresh fruits, assorted cheeses and delectable pastries, courtesy of the city's best patisserie, had more than made up for the pain of waking up early on her Saturday off and driving to Marula Heights to join Donald for brunch.

'So, what's on your agenda today?' River wiped her fingers on her napkin and returned her attention to the man sitting across from her at the enormous dining table while Monica carried away the used plates.

Donald swallowed the remaining drops of his black coffee and shrugged. 'I've got some scripts for a new television show to go through and a couple of virtual meetings this afternoon with a production company in the States.'

'That sounds exciting. Are you planning to produce a show like *Start the Music* in America?' she asked curiously. Donald had a multiplicity of business interests and from what she could fathom from the little he chose to share, his television productions and music shows seemed to take up most of his time and attention.

'I'd prefer not to go into the details of my business affairs,' he said flatly. 'I'm sure there are other things we can discuss.'

Taken aback by the abrupt response, River shrugged in turn. 'Fine, have it your way. I was only trying to show an interest. If you trust me enough to ask me to move in with you, I don't know why your work has to be such a mystery.'

Purposely ignoring her comment, Donald glanced at his watch and then looked at her enquiringly. 'What are your plans for your day off?'

She bit back her frustration at the high-handed attitude and kept her voice even. 'I've got some office paperwork at home to deal with and then I've promised Sly I'd go with him to look at some apartments this afternoon. His lease is almost up, and he wants my opinion on a few places he's seen.'

'Don't you do enough of that when you're at work?'

'I know, right?' River laughed. 'But Sly is my best friend so it's not like I have a choice.'

'Well, actually, you do,' Donald said pointedly. There was no trace of humour in his face and River looked at him uncertainly.

'I don't mind doing it, Donald. Sly has always been there for me and anyway, you know I love looking at properties.'

'Well, since you don't mind mixing work and pleasure and we both agree I'm rather more important than your little puppy dog, I could use your professional input on a property I'm looking at for my new office. I'll be taking on more staff soon and there isn't enough space at the

Airport office. We can go this afternoon.'

River stared at him in astonishment. 'But you've just said you have your whole day planned! What about the meetings you've arranged with the people in the States?'

She paused as Monica came back into the room and stacked up the remaining dishes and as soon as the housekeeper left the room, River exploded. 'What exactly is your problem with me going out with Sly? This isn't the first nasty comment you've made about him and you don't even know him. Must I remind you that he's my *friend*?'

'Yes, and I'm your *man*. Of course, I have no problem with you seeing your friends, but it's not unreasonable to expect that you put me first when I need your help, is it?'

He clearly felt no need to justify his change of plans and infuriated by the devious manoeuvre and his intransigence, River glared at him furiously. Of course, she couldn't say no to Donald, even though they both knew he would probably disregard any opinions she offered. She had yet to hear Donald ask for anyone's advice about anything, and her own experience of selling him a property proved he was already a master dealmaker.

Donald pushed his chair back and stood up. 'I'll be in the study. Enjoy the rest of your morning and I'll send you a message when I've confirmed the appointment time for the viewing.'

For a moment River itched to punch the satisfied smile off his face and then disgusted with herself for giving in, she nodded and watched him leave the room. So much for my great negotiation skills, she thought gloomily. She rested her elbows on the empty table and cupped her face in her hands, certain of only one thing. *Sly is going to be furious!*

* * *

'Give me one good reason why you're ditching me again at the last minute.'

When she couldn't immediately answer, Sly sounded incredulous. 'Do you know how long it's taken me to line up these appointments so we can do everything in one afternoon? After all, it's not like my best friend who just happens to rent and sell property for a living has bothered to help me find a new home.'

River winced as the jab hit home. Sly's budget was far too small for her to justify the time and effort required. None of the properties she handled now went for less than ten million cedis and Harvey would have killed her for wasting Premier's time on scouring the market for studios and one-bedroom rentals. As far as Harvey was concerned, family and friends were not to be confused with paying clients.

Sly wasn't finished. 'I know I'm not at your usual millionaire level, but this is outside your work time and the least you can do is keep your promise to me as your *friend*. I have to put down a rent advance on one of these places by next week and I need your help to pick the right one and negotiate a rent I can actually afford. *Please*, River!'

River was close to tears at the naked desperation in his voice. 'I'm so sorry, Sly. I wouldn't cancel on you unless it was important. But Donald needs—'

'So, let me understand this. Because Donald has suddenly decided he wants you to do something for him, *I* just get dumped. Is this how it's always going to be?'

'Sly, please don't make this harder for me than it already is,' she pleaded. 'You're very important to me. You're my best friend, for God's sake!'

'I warned you that man would come between us, didn't I?'

'Look, I don't blame you for being angry with me, but it's got nothing to do with Donald. It's all my fault. He – he asked me ages ago, and I completely forgot. Instead of agreeing to come with you when you asked me, I should—' she broke off before she did any further damage. Lying to Sly was a big mistake.

Sly's voice sounded like chipped ice. 'Yeah, stop right there, River. I'm not an idiot so don't make it worse by lying to me. I thought after what happened with Cameron that you'd learned your lesson. I honestly don't know who you are anymore. You really don't care who you hurt so long as it's not the great provider, Donald Ayo! I'm asking you as your best friend to do *one* thing for me, but all you care about is pleasing a man you can't even bring yourself to sleep with.'

'Sly, I'm sorry. *Please* don't be angry with me,' she begged.

For a moment he was silent and then, 'Well I can't pretend I didn't see this coming. First Cameron, and now me.'

'Sly, listen to me, I'll go with you another time, I promise. You know what, I'll talk to some people and help you find a new place...' she tailed off miserably, aware that whatever she offered now was too little and much too late.

***

Later that afternoon, River sat silently in the passenger seat of Donald's Mercedes, unable to get the awful scene with Sly out of her head. She shot a resentful glance at Donald, but his attention was on the road and any emotion was shielded behind his sunglasses. Not that he would care about her upset feelings anyway, River thought bitterly. His only reaction when she'd tearfully reported her fallout with Sly was an indifferent shrug and a caustic reminder that she should focus on friends who could take her forward in life. After everything Sly had done for her, she had let down her best friend again, and for what? A brief tour of an uninspiring office block conducted by a flustered estate agent who'd clearly been drafted in at the last minute. It had been obvious to all three of them within ten minutes that the floor space available was inadequate, and after directing a few perfunctory questions at the agent, Donald had shepherded River back to the car. And now, even if she had the temerity to try, it was too late in the day to call Sly and offer her help.

River looked through the window at the passing scenery and wondered whether the bargain she had struck with the man beside her was worth the high price she was paying. She and Sly had had each other's backs since childhood and there had never been a time – day or night – when he hadn't been there if she needed him. Her heart ached for him and for the pain she had caused by putting someone else ahead of their friendship. Nothing and no one, not even Cameron, had ever come between them. Until now. Until Donald.

Chapter 15

The quiet ticking of the large silver-framed clock on the wall was the only sound in the hallway when River used the key Donald had given her to let herself into his house and shut the door. The empty space in the forecourt had already signalled that he wasn't yet home and there was no sign of life. Monica was no doubt in her self-contained quarters behind the main house as with her boss scheduled to attend a dinner party that evening, there had been no need to prepare his dinner.

River stood with her back pressed against the solid wood of the front door and tried to summon the energy she would need for the evening. But, in truth, she was drained from a long day packed with viewings and would have given anything for a quiet dinner at home, and preferably her home rather than Donald's. Sly was still refusing to take her calls and she felt sick whenever she thought of their quarrel. She also felt intensely lonely. After the break-up with Cameron, River had shied away from their mutual friends, initially because she dreaded stumbling across Cameron – or Cameron and Nina as it now was. Later, when Donald began commandeering River's free time, it became easier to make excuses for not meeting up with her crowd and slowly drifting away from her tight-knit group of friends. Over the past two weeks it had become painfully clear that Sly's warning about her ending up with no friends was no more than the truth. Even Sefa, the only person she could still confide in, was buried in the extensive reading list from the MBA programme she had signed on to and didn't have time to keep her company.

With her long evening gown swishing gently around her legs, River walked slowly into the hallway. Without the benefit of sunshine coming through the atrium, the house was dark and felt gloomy. For the first time, the beautiful house couldn't heal the raw pain lodged in River's heart as she contemplated the loss of her best friend. It wasn't hard to see the irony of breaking up with Cameron to prove her strength and independence, only to let Donald manipulate her to the point where she was now alone. Contemplating how she had ended up in her situation, River knew it was time to face the truth she'd buried beneath layers of pride, self-justification, and greed. She, who had always considered honesty as expendable, stood in the silent hallway and forced herself to pull off the blinkers she had chosen to wear for months, recognising how gradually but inexorably Donald Ayo had come to control everything about her. She couldn't remember when she had stopped wearing trousers, finding it easier to give in to Donald's preference that she stick to skirts and the dresses he chose for her. Donald had become the arbiter of everything from her hairstyle to the car she drove. Undeterred by his shameless attempt to prise her away from her job at Premier, it was Donald who had successfully manipulated her into severing her friendships, first with the girlfriends he had dubbed 'unserious', and now with her beloved Sly. And what burned River the most was that *she* had allowed it to happen.

As dusk turned into night, the hallway grew darker and eventually River moved to the wall and flicked the switch. The room was instantly flooded with light and she gazed around at the beautiful columns and graceful archways of her dream house. Dreams really aren't all they appear to be, she thought sadly, tracing the silky magnolia walls with her fingertips. Donald's house *was* beautiful but there was no warmth, no heart, no love to be found here. Instead of the happiness she had sought, being with Donald had only brought her misery. It was time to end things before it was too late.

Lost in her thoughts, the sound of the gate swinging open and Donald's powerful Mercedes sweeping up the driveway didn't register, and it wasn't until he opened the door and walked in that she snapped out of her daze.

'Hey, River, I'm so sorry I'm late! The traffic was even worse than usual. I'll change quickly and then we can go.' Even after a long day at work, Donald looked immaculate and River watched in silence as he came up to her and kissed her cheeks.

He took in her expression and frowned in bewilderment. 'Why are you standing here looking so sad? Are you unwell?'

Feeling utterly desolate, she tried to speak but somehow the words seemed to stick in her throat. She took a deep breath and tried again. 'Donald, listen, I need to be honest with you. I—'

Before she could say another word, he pulled her into his arms and kissed her. River instinctively tried to pull away, but he wouldn't let her and after a moment she stopped resisting. Suddenly curious to see whether his kiss could spark emotion into a heart which had felt numb for months, she gave herself up to the sensation of his warm lips moving over hers, relaxing as his hands urgently caressed her back before sliding up to stroke her neck and cup her face.

When he eventually lifted his head, she stared up at him with wide eyes and her heart pounding.

'Donald—'

'Shh...' He placed a finger over her lips, once again preventing her from speaking, and his eyes glittered with an emotion she couldn't place.

'You have to forgive me, River. I've taken you – us – for granted. Listen, I know what I've said in the past, but things change.'

She shook her head dumbly, but still he held her captive, his voice suddenly urgent. 'My darling, I'll call your parents tomorrow and make an appointment to visit. After all, it's only proper I tell them to their face that I want to marry their daughter.'

River pushed his hand away from her mouth and stared at him in disbelief. '*What* did you say?'

Donald's answer was to pull her against him and slide his arms down her back, holding her firmly against him and linking his hands at the base of her spine. Then he leaned his forehead against hers and murmured, 'Marry me, River.'

* * *

The room was humming with the sound of chatter while music from the live band stationed on the verandah drifted through the open French doors.

What the hell am I doing here? River forced a smile and shook hands with the couple Donald was introducing, barely registering their names as she tried to make sense of how her attempt at finishing things with Donald had ended with her accompanying him to a birthday celebration for the wife of a government minister. Between her shock at Donald's sudden declaration and her guilt about ending the relationship, however toxic it had become, River had found herself agreeing to postpone any further discussion until after the dinner party.

The conversation quickly turned to politics and bored by the same old arguments, River's attention wandered around the sizeable living space, her professional instincts taking over as she appraised the expensive artwork displayed under spotlights strategically studded around the high ceilings. The room and its furnishings were beautiful, but River would still have preferred to be at home. Suppressing a sigh, she turned her attention back to the people in front of her. Donald and his friend were still animatedly discussing the forthcoming elections and River exchanged wry glances with the man's wife. The woman, who River vaguely remembered Donald introducing as Linda, grasped River's arm to take her aside.

'You must give me your card,' Linda said in a low voice and leaned in closer, almost overpowering River with the cloying sweetness of her perfume. 'I hear you're in real estate and we're thinking about selling our beach house. To be honest with you, I've had terrible experiences with estate agents in the past and I would prefer to use someone we know.'

'Of course.' River smiled politely, feeling none of her old excitement at the prospect of a wealthy new client. Reaching into her bag, she extracted one of the gold-embossed business cards Harvey insisted she never left home without. 'Please give me a call whenever you're ready.'

Linda reached for the card and her eyes locked on to River's handbag. 'That is gorgeous!' she exclaimed. 'It's a Fendi, isn't it?'

River nodded and automatically held up the leather baguette with its prominent gold clasp. Linda scrutinised it and then looked at River appraisingly. 'You're very lucky to have a man like Donald Ayo. I don't know him well, but I hear he's very generous.'

With a furtive glance at Donald and her husband, both still deep in conversation, Linda lowered her voice to a whisper. 'You know, my dear, I've been with Nelson for almost ten years and he takes good care of me. If you've managed to capture Donald, do *whatever* it takes to keep him happy. Follow my advice and you will never be short of designer bags.'

She tapped the side of her nose in a conspiratorial fashion and giggled, and the high-pitched sound grated on River's nerves almost as much as the insinuation behind the woman's words. Suddenly desperate for fresh air and solitude, River excused herself and left the room. Out on the terrace, the band had taken a short break and she wandered to the far end of the flagstone porch, breathing in the fragrant night air while trying to calm her turbulent thoughts. The beautiful, landscaped garden was like the setting of a fairytale with outdoor lamps illuminating the grounds and strings of twinkling fairy lights threaded through the thick foliage of the surrounding bushes and trees.

Yet, the beauty of her surroundings did nothing to diminish the dread churning in her stomach as she contemplated how to end the relationship with Donald. She was only too aware that doing so would bring consequences and while part of her defiantly wondered what more he could do to her after ruining her relationship with Cameron and alienating her best friend, River was also smart enough to know that rejecting a man as powerful and successful as Donald Ayo was likely to exact a heavy price.

Chapter 16

The band had returned to their spot on the terrace and River was heading inside when she heard someone call her name and turned to see Jerry Andoh walking towards her.

'I *knew* it was you!' Jerry beamed as he kissed her warmly on both cheeks. He turned to the woman by his side and gestured towards River. 'This is the lady from Premier Properties who is selling the house. You know, Donald Ayo's friend.'

Turning back to River, he added, 'My dear, let me introduce you to my wife, Cynthia.'

Jerry's good humour was infectious and despite her inner turmoil, River greeted his wife with a warm smile. 'It's a pleasure to meet you, Mrs Andoh. I was beginning to think Jerry was making you up.'

On all River's visits to Jerry's house for viewings with prospective buyers or to report to him on progress with the sale, Cynthia was invariably delayed by a beauty appointment of some kind and the two women had never met. While the woman's make-up was flawless and her nails perfectly manicured, the brittle society matron River had imagined Cynthia Andoh to be was a far cry from the short, plump woman with warm, twinkly eyes who ignored River's outstretched hand and instead hugged her warmly.

The three of them had been chatting for a few minutes when Donald suddenly appeared by River's side and placed a proprietary arm around her shoulders. 'So, this is where you've been hiding! I've been looking everywhere for you.'

River instinctively shrank from his touch, but Donald didn't appear to notice as he greeted Jerry with a handshake and leaned down to kiss Cynthia. River was anxious to say her piece and get the evening over with, but any hopes that Donald was ready to leave were dashed when he nodded in the direction of the garden and gave her shoulder a gentle squeeze.

'Mercy has asked that we take our seats for dinner so let's find a table and get you a drink, shall we? Jerry, why don't you and Cynthia sit with us?'

With that, Donald took the lead and River reluctantly followed with Jerry and Cynthia close behind as they went out onto the terrace and down a flight of stone steps. Tables draped in crisp white linen cloths and chairs had been arranged on the lawn flanked by long trestle tables carrying large steel chafing dishes for the buffet dinner. Stopping at one of the tables, Donald pulled out a chair for River and she reluctantly sat down, sorely regretting ever agreeing to come. As soon as Cynthia and Jerry were settled, Donald beckoned to a passing waiter who brought over a chilled bottle of white wine and swiftly filled everyone's glasses.

'Good health, my friends!' Donald raised his glass and the others followed suit. Taking a quick swallow, he put down his drink and clasped River's hand possessively.

'So, Cynthia, now you've finally met each other, what do you think of my fiancée?'

River promptly choked on the wine she was drinking, while Cynthia, who was sitting next to her, stared at her with wide eyes.

'Wait, *fiancée*?' Looking bemused, Cynthia turned back to her husband. 'But Jerry, why didn't you say so when you introduced her?'

Her husband responded with a shrug of bewilderment which Cynthia greeted with an impatient tut before patting River's arm warmly. 'Congratulations, my dear! I hope you don't mind me saying that many women have tried to tame this man and I was beginning to think he would be a bachelor for ever. I don't know what magic you've worked on him, but well done!'

Recovering quickly, Jerry blew an extravagant kiss across to River and grinned widely. 'I had no idea but yes, congratulations to you both! Donald, I hope you know you are a very lucky man.'

Jerry's compliment did nothing to appease River and she glared at Donald, outraged by the extent of his audacity. *What the hell!* He knew perfectly well she hadn't agreed to his proposal and that she was only at the dinner on the understanding they would discuss things after the party.

Donald, however, appeared perfectly relaxed as he picked up his wine glass and calmly took a sip. 'We make our own luck, Jerry, but I have to agree I'm very fortunate.'

Only the arrival of other guests at their table made River swallow the heated words trembling on her lips. She responded to their murmured greetings and gulped the rest of the wine in her glass as she struggled to control her fury. Once again, she had allowed Donald to seize control of the situation. Despite his earlier assurances, he was obviously counting on her to go along with his bold announcement or risk making them both look foolish. When the waiter arrived to serve drinks to the new arrivals, River held out her empty glass and tossed back half the contents as soon as he'd refilled it. Sensing Donald was watching her, River deliberately took another long sip and then stared at him defiantly, feeling a savage satisfaction at the uneasy expression that flickered across face.

'Take it easy, we have a long night ahead of us,' he murmured, but she turned away, too angry and frustrated to speak to him. Cynthia's attention was on the new arrival who had taken the seat next to her and as River looked around the table at the well-dressed couples chatting easily among themselves, unexpected tears pricked the back of her eyes. No one at their table looked under forty and seeing how comfortable they all appeared to be with each other, she was overcome by an intense feeling of loneliness. *Be careful what you wish for, River.* After all the years spent scrimping and saving her money while dreaming of the day she could enjoy the lifestyle of the rich and famous, her wish had been granted and she had already had her fill of high society. She had no interest in being half of a high-profile power couple and playing the part Donald was trying to force her into. Quite the contrary. Now surrounded by the people she had once aspired to be, River would have gladly handed over her house fund money for the chance to be back in Kwame's no-frills restaurant sharing kebabs with Cameron and enjoying beer with Sly and her girlfriends.

'So, when is the wedding?' Cynthia's excited voice cut into River's thoughts. She was saved from responding by the band striking up a rousing rendition of *Happy Birthday* to herald the entrance of the hosts. Everyone rose to clap vigorously as Lucas Peterson, the handsome government minister widely tipped as a future presidential candidate, escorted his beautifully dressed wife to the high table. River watched enviously as Mercy Peterson smiled sweetly at her guests before taking her seat. *Well, at least someone's happy.*

Dinner passed in a blur of polite conversation and River helped herself to several more glasses of wine. Cynthia's attention had been largely monopolised by the woman sitting beside her, sparing River from any further awkward questions. But after the waiter cleared their plates, Cynthia's neighbour, who had apparently just been brought up to speed on the latest gossip, leaned forward. The band was on a short break and as a result the woman's voice carried clearly.

'Donald Ayo! What is this I'm hearing? *You* are actually getting *married*?'

While River groaned silently and stared down at the table, wishing herself a million miles away, Donald seemed unperturbed and draped an arm over her shoulders to draw her against him. Forcing herself not to pull away while everyone's eyes were on them, River contented herself with giving him a sidelong glance and mentally willing him to deny everything. Unfortunately, Donald – unlike River – was enjoying the attention.

'Dora, you're putting me on the spot here,' he drawled with an easy smile. 'I hadn't planned on making any announcements tonight and this beautiful woman beside me is very shy.'

'Answer the question,' Dora chided with an impish smile. 'Because let me tell you, I must hear this from your own lips.'

Just say no! The wine River had been drinking so liberally began to churn unpleasantly in her stomach, and she gritted her teeth. Despite the humid warmth of the night, her skin was suddenly cold and clammy and Donald's arm resting across her shoulders felt like a dead weight trapping her in her seat. Only too aware of how manipulative the man beside her could be, she held her breath and waited, knowing even before he spoke what Donald was about to do.

'Very well. I didn't want to embarrass River because she's not used to all this attention and it's something we've only just decided, but yes, we're getting married.' With an apologetic smile at River, Donald injected a note of pleading into his voice. 'Forgive me for sharing our news sooner than we'd planned, but can you blame me for telling the world how happy you've made me?'

Everyone's eyes swung from Donald to River and a rush of nausea washed over her. She swallowed hard and opened her mouth, but when no words emerged, the silence stretched out uncomfortably. Utterly mortified by the curious expressions forming on the faces around the table, she could feel Donald's fingers tighten painfully around her shoulder. But even knowing he was simply playing to the gallery, she still couldn't force out the words he wanted her to say.

Cynthia nudged River gently and then leaned in to

ask softly, 'Is everything all right, my dear?'

The kind words broke River out of her state of paralysis. Shrugging off Donald's arm and ignoring the flash of fury that crossed his face, she pushed back her chair and stood up abruptly. 'I'm... I'm so sorry... I don't feel very well...'

Grabbing her bag from the table, she ducked her head and ran for the house, tears of shame and despair cascading down her cheeks as she weaved her way between the tables to reach the terrace.

There was no sign of life in the hallway and River slowed to dash an impatient hand across her wet cheeks before heading towards the front door. Her chest heaved painfully from the tears she had suppressed for months and she was desperate to get away. Just as she wrenched open the front door, she heard Donald's voice behind her. In a blind panic, she dashed out of the door and started down the tree-lined driveway leading to the front gates.

'River, *wait!*'

The constraints of her floor-length strapless gown and high heels were no match for Donald's long strides and within moments he was in front of her, grasping her arm to stop her fleeing.

'What the *hell* are you playing at?' he demanded, his voice thick with rage. 'How dare you humiliate me in front of everyone?'

'What am *I* playing at?' she panted furiously, blinking away the tears. '*You* shouldn't have made an announcement in front of everyone when I haven't even agreed to marry you.'

'Let's not waste time pretending you won't accept my proposal. Where else are you going to get an offer like this?'

She glared at him, almost breathless with anger. 'How *dare* you? Are – are you so arrogant that you think no woman could possibly say no to you?'

Donald yanked her arm and pulled her roughly against him until his face was almost touching hers. 'I *chose* you, River, and I've done more for you than for any other woman,' he snarled savagely. 'Aren't I the one who brought you business and gave you a decent car to drive? Dammit, I even bought this bloody dress you're wearing! I've shown you a good time without making any demands on you, and now – now when I'm offering us the chance to have a great life together in a beautiful mansion any woman would die for, *this* is how you choose to repay me?'

He sounded so menacing that River forced herself to take a deep breath to calm her ragged breathing while she scrabbled to defuse the tension before things got out of hand. This was not how she had wanted to end things, but there was also no turning back now. Wary of inflaming the situation further, she chose her words carefully.

'I'm very grateful for all the things you've done for me, Donald, and I've told you so many times. But I also know that I could never love you. You've been very kind and generous, and you deserve someone who genuinely cares for you.'

Releasing her, he stared at her dispassionately. 'I know exactly what I want and what I deserve, River. I told you the first time I met you that you're different. We make a great couple and you'd be lying if you said otherwise.'

Donald's infuriating high-handedness combined with the wine she had consumed tossed River's attempts at diplomacy overboard. 'Okay, Donald, if you want the truth, then let's have it. *You* don't love me either. Yes, you chose me, but it wasn't for *me*, not really. What you're looking for is an accessory for your perfect house and your perfect life.'

He raised an eyebrow and she rushed on. 'Be honest, is it really me you want or is all this just to prove to yourself that you can have me or anyone *you* choose? It's interesting you mentioned our first meeting because do you know what I think? I think you were only interested in me when you knew I had a boyfriend – when I suddenly became someone you could compete with Cameron over.'

'Don't be ridiculous! I was attracted to you from the moment I saw you.'

River's laugh was bitter and held no trace of humour. 'Really? Then, if it's me you want, why have you tried to change *everything* about me? Yes, you've bought me clothes, but it's only so I dress the way you want me to. The only reason you gave me that car to drive is because you don't consider my office car good enough for the great Donald Ayo's girlfriend. I can't even wear my hair in a style I'm comfortable with because it's not sophisticated enough for you. You want to control me, not love me!'

'And, of course, *you* came to me out of love, right?' he said sardonically, and River flushed.

'I suppose I deserve that,' she conceded. 'But it doesn't change anything about what I've just said. Maybe I didn't love you, but at least I was honest about who I was.'

'*Honest?*' His voice was thick with contempt. 'Is that

what you call starting a relationship with a man just because of his house? I mean, who does that, River? Isn't there a name for girls like you?'

The sharp sound of the slap reverberated in the dusky gloom. In the electric silence that followed, River gasped aloud and covered her mouth with a hand still shaking from the stinging blow she had just inflicted.

'The truth hurts, doesn't it?' Donald remarked, flexing his jaw gingerly. 'I was right when I called you wild, wasn't I? But this time you've picked the wrong person.'

He lunged forward and grabbed her arm and his grip felt as cold and inflexible as steel. Instead of panic, River felt only pent-up fury and frustration surge through her, and she fought back, scratching viciously at his face with her free arm. Taken aback by the ferocity of her attack, Donald's grip loosened, allowing her to wrench her arm out of his hold and step away from him.

He growled and came for her again and she screamed so loudly that he stopped in his tracks. Taking advantage of his hesitation, River slid her chunky Fendi baguette off her shoulder and seizing the chain, she swung the bag hard at him, all the while shrieking insults at him that she hadn't realised she knew. The solid metal clasp connected forcefully with his cheek and he staggered backwards.

'*Madam! Madam!*'

The sight of two security men running up the path towards them stopped Donald in his tracks, and seizing her opportunity, River gathered up the skirt of her dress and raced towards them. When she reached the safety of the guards, she turned around to see Donald striding rapidly back towards the house.

River promptly burst into tears while the two men stood by helplessly, murmuring quietly to each other. When one of the guards tentatively suggested calling the boss, River gulped down her sobs and shook her head emphatically. The last thing she wanted was to draw any further attention to herself. After exchanging glances, the guards escorted her to the gate where she thanked them with a shaky smile before walking out on to the road. Other than the security detail guarding the luxury cars lined up outside the house, the area was deserted. She ignored the curious glances from the uniformed guards and leaned against a Range Rover parked on the verge, traumatised by her violent encounter with Donald.

She had never been in any kind of physical altercation before and suddenly it was all too much. Not caring who could see her, River hunched her shoulders and sobbed uncontrollably. She was crying so hard that it was only when her sobs subsided that it dawned on her she was stranded. Her – or rather Donald's – Mercedes was parked in his driveway and she had left the keys on top of the cabinet in his hallway. Although even the thought of driving Donald's car, or having anything at all to do with him, made her feel sick, it didn't change the fact that Marula Heights was a private residential estate and there were no commercial taxis to be seen. River had never felt so lonely, and fresh tears tumbled down her cheeks. She gulped down the sobs that threatened to overwhelm her and fumbled in her bag for her phone. With trembling fingers, she punched out a number while muttering feverishly under her breath, 'Please pick up, *please* pick up.'

This time he answered her call and almost hysterical with relief, River couldn't stop babbling. 'Please, *please,* I'm really scared. I'm out here on a road all alone. I'm *so* sorry for everything. *Please* come and get me!'

For a moment there was silence and then Sly said grimly, 'Tell me where you are. I'm on my way.'

Chapter 17

The rain lashing against the office window behind her mirrored the bleakness of River's spirits. Even the relative peace of her own private space created by the screens around her desk area which Harvey optimistically described as an office, didn't raise her spirits. As she flipped idly through the surveyor's report on one of her sale properties, she paused at the reference to damp in the bedrooms and sighed; the buyer would now almost certainly demand a reduction in price. But even the prospect of haggling, normally her favourite part of the sales process, today felt tedious. Although it was over three months since the shocking end to her relationship with Donald, on some days it was still proving a struggle to find her sparkle.

On that fateful night, true to his word, Sly had broken every speed limit to rescue her from outside the Minister's house, driving her straight back to his apartment where he had sat with her until she finally cried herself to sleep. It was Sly who had phoned Harvey to explain that River was too distraught to come in and wouldn't be at work for a few days, before calling his own boss to plead illness. It was also Sly who had eventually driven River home and broken the news to her parents about the events of the previous night, pleading with her father not to report Donald's attempted assault to the police to spare his daughter further pain.

That night had been the final straw for River. The trauma brought on by the attack had demolished the barriers she had erected around her emotions since throwing in her lot with Donald Ayo. Racked with remorse at letting the music mogul dominate her life and manipulate her friendships, River was finally forced to confront the pain of losing Cameron which she had tried so hard to bury. Constantly tearful and emotionally fragile, it had taken weeks before Sly's attentiveness, Harvey's support at work, and the relentless cosseting of her family had helped to ease the worst of River's torment.

River jumped as an ear-splitting clap of lightning was followed by a deep rumble of thunder, and she swivelled her chair around to peer through the window. The rainy season was in full swing and the fat raindrops slapping against the glass showed no sign of abating. It was lucky she had no viewings scheduled as this was hardly the weather to entice anyone into buying a house.

'Are you ready for this?'

River turned around to see a grinning Harvey standing in front of her desk, one hand hidden behind his back. She smiled at his excited expression and wondered what her boss had up his sleeve this time. Undeterred by River's constant assurances, Harvey had taken to offering unexpected incentives to forestall any temptation she might feel to jump ship and leave Premier Properties.

'Ready for what?' She looked at him enquiringly, hoping he wasn't about to spring another weekend trip to Cape Coast on her. She still hadn't forgiven Sly for his disgraceful antics at Coconut Grove during their last freebie.

'Ta-da!' Harvey swung his arm forward with a flourish and River leaned over her desk to pluck the slip of paper he was brandishing.

'Oh!' she exclaimed, stunned into silence by the figure scrawled on the form. Dumbly she looked up at Harvey and he rubbed his hands together and nodded enthusiastically.

'That's your commission on the Andoh town house. I wanted you to have it a-sarp. I've doubled the usual percentage to recognise all the work and... err... the trouble you took to make the sale happen during such a... err... well, you know, a difficult time.'

River smiled wryly at Harvey's earnest attempts at diplomacy. Her boss still tiptoed cautiously around the subject of Donald Ayo which, she conceded, was understandable given the mess she had been for weeks afterwards.

River scrutinised the figures scribbled on the remittance note and ran through some rapid mental calculations. *Oh my God, I've done it!* A wide smile spread across her face, immediately lifting her gloomy spirits. Thanks to Harvey's generous commission, she now had enough money saved for a sizeable deposit on a property. For a moment she sat there speechless, trying to comprehend that she had finally achieved what had so often felt impossible. *I've hit my house fund target!*

Then springing to her feet and heedless of the transparent Perspex screens which made her visible to the rest of the staff in the open-plan office, River impulsively dashed around her desk and hugged her boss tightly. 'Harvey, I don't even know what to say.

Thank you so *so* much... you honestly don't know what this means to me!'

Harvey patted her back, looking pleased, but awkward. 'You deserve it, River. You've worked hard and brought us a lot of business in these challenging times.'

Spotting some of the other sales staff openly gawking at the improbable sight of someone embracing the boss, Harvey disentangled himself and raised his voice. 'As you know, River, at Premier we always reward those who do a good job and who... *focus on their work.*'

Taking the hint, his staff reluctantly returned to their activities and Harvey winked at River. 'Keep up the good work.' As he turned to leave, his brows shot up at the sight of an elaborate flower arrangement sitting on top of River's filing cabinet.

River followed his gaze and grinned. 'Aren't they something? They're a thank you gift from Cynthia Andoh. She's really happy in their new house – and apparently it's a lot closer to her hairdresser.'

* * *

'River, Sly's here!' Sefa's voice, followed by the sound of the front door slamming, carried upstairs and through River's half-open bedroom door.

'I'll be down in two minutes!' River yelled back and resumed her task of emptying out the contents of her handbag onto her bed to find her house keys.

She pulled open a drawer in search of an evening bag and her eyes fell on the small designer bag pushed to the back which she must have missed when she'd packed and returned the dresses and gifts Donald had given her. There was a small dent in the Fendi's classic shape which immediately recalled the violent end to Mercy Peterson's birthday party. Reluctant to destroy an expensive accessory, she made a mental note to donate the bag to Sefa and pulled out her trusty Prada, stuffing it with a stick of lip gloss and her mobile phone.

She stood in front of the mirror for a final check and tucked the lacy white top she'd chosen into her favourite black jeans, still a little loose from the weight she'd lost over the past weeks. Giving her curls a final fluff, she sighed with satisfaction. Liberating her hair from the sophisticated chignons and pinned-back styles Donald had favoured was one of many things she was enjoying since finishing with him.

River skipped downstairs and into the living room, arriving just in time to rescue Sly from Auntie Mansa before she launched into a full-blown description of her latest ailment. Within minutes they were in Sly's car and gunning down the highway towards Kwame's restaurant.

'Seriously, your family is something else!' Sly was still chuckling as he turned off the beach road and drove down an untarred track leading to a large car park.

'Tell me about it,' River agreed. 'I love them dearly but as much as I'll miss seeing Sefa every day, I really need my own space. Thanks for agreeing to come house-hunting with me this weekend, I honestly cannot wait to start looking at houses.'

Sly turned off the engine and River opened the door and stepped out of the car, taking a moment to breathe in the fresh evening air. The downpour earlier that day had brought some welcome relief from the usual sticky humidity of the tropical nights. She cast an almost-casual look around the car park but there was no sign of Cameron's pick-up. Even though she and Sly had been begun to frequent Kwame's joint again, they hadn't once run into Cameron which, she assured herself, was perfectly all right with her.

'Hey, welcome you guys!' Kwame hurried towards them armed with two menus as soon as he spotted Sly and River entering the restaurant. River hugged him warmly and then she giggled and pointed a teasing finger at his stomach. 'When's it due?'

Kwame enjoyed eating his kebabs as much as selling them and his widening girth had become a running joke between them. She shrieked with laughter as he aimed a mock blow at her before flinging his arm across her shoulders and pulling her against him with a smile. Releasing her, Kwame shook hands with Sly and led them to a table overlooking the beach.

The instant they were seated, Kwame handed over the menus, his eyes twinkling with mischief. 'Guess who left here literally ten minutes ago?'

River's eyes widened as she stared up at him. 'Oh my God, *really*? I was just thinking it's so weird how we've never run into each other here.'

Sly cast a cursory look at the menu Kwame had handed him and then tossed it onto the table. 'I don't know why you bother with menus when we always order the same thing.' He raised an eyebrow at River's impatient expression. '*What*?'

'Didn't you hear what Kwame said? Cameron was just here!'

'I see him all the time. He's always at the gallery with Nina these days. His exhibition kicks off next week, remember?'

Kwame pointed to the bare wall behind their table. 'He came to collect the last of the paintings he lent me, and I've made him promise to paint a special one to replace it. After this exhibition, his career's going to take off big time, which means his work will be worth a fortune in a few years. Mind you,' he looked directly at River, 'it's probably a good thing you didn't bump into him, seeing as he was here with Nina. Not that you'd care or anything?'

River gave a casual shrug and pretended to be engrossed in her menu. Of course, she cared but she was damned if she would let either of the men present know it. Kwame and Cameron were as close as brothers and she didn't need Kwame reporting back to Cam that River was still pining for him. Her ex-boyfriend had clearly moved on and she couldn't face any further humiliation.

After placing their food order, River and Sly sat in companionable silence sipping beer and looking through the window at the darkness of the sea. In the dusk, all that was visible were the white flecks of foam from the waves crashing onto the beach a few metres away. After a few minutes, Sly turned to look at River and when she met his eyes in silent enquiry, he hesitated.

'What is it?' she asked curiously.

'I dunno... I was just thinking about what you said about not having run into Cameron. What about Donald Ayo? Have you heard anything from him?'

River stiffened, and then took a quick sip of her beer.

'Not a word, thank God!' She thumped her glass onto the table for emphasis.

There had been no contact from Donald since the night of the party and recalling his many meetings related to his business in America, River occasionally wondered if he had travelled abroad. There had been no acknowledgement of the clothes and other gifts she had sent back to his house by taxi and neither Jerry nor Cynthia Andoh had mentioned his name throughout the weeks she had managed their house sale. River had also soon discovered that losing her access to the exclusive circles she had mixed in when she was with Donald had in no way hurt Premier's business. Much to River's surprise, Linda – the woman who had asked for her card at Mercy's birthday party – had eventually called to make an appointment, even passing on River's details to a friend who was house-hunting. All of which brought River the added satisfaction of knowing her pipeline of new clients was now due to her reputation for excellence and not the man she was dating.

Sly had been staring at her expectantly and River grimaced. 'Why are you asking about Donald, anyway?'

'I'm just curious, that's all, and I want to know you're okay. Do you still think about him? I know *I* do, and I'd love to kick him where it hurts for what he did to you.'

River smiled faintly. 'That's very sweet of you, my hero, but the only thing that hurts a man like Donald is losing his pride and having his public image dented. Which means he's suffering big time without you having to lift a finger. The man is so arrogant that I'm pretty sure having a woman walk out on him in front of his friends at such a high-profile dinner hit him harder than either of us could do. I knew I'd be in trouble for dumping him – after all, *no one* humiliates the great Donald Ayo and gets away with it. That's why he turned so savage and was ready to beat me up. My only consolation is thinking how mortifying it must have been for him to go back in there without me and with a massive bruise above his eye after announcing to everyone we were getting married!'

After munching their way through several skewers of kebabs and getting through another round of beers, River leaned back in her chair and smiled happily as she wiped her greasy lips with a paper napkin.

'It's good to see you back to your old self again,' Sly said, looking amused.

'I know,' she agreed ruefully. 'I still can't get over how I let that man get into my head so badly.'

'Forget about him. You've faced your demons – and no question that Ayo man is the devil himself – and come through it. But while we're talking about the men in your past, I really think you should come to the opening night party for Cameron's exhibition.'

River looked at him in horror. 'Why the hell would I do that?'

'To show that you're over him and you're ready to make peace and move on? Or at least that's what you keep insisting, so prove it by coming. I'll be there, and Aku and the girls have all said they're coming. Go on, it'll be fun!'

'Isn't the opening party supposed to be the hottest ticket in town? The last I heard it was completely sold out.' She shrugged as nonchalantly as if her pulse wasn't suddenly racing and she didn't feel tingly all over.

Sly looked hard at her, a shrewd glint in his eyes. 'My friend, I *work* at the gallery. If you want to come, you won't need a ticket. So, what do you say?'

Chapter 18

River stood in the doorway of the packed art gallery, stunned by the sheer number of people. Whatever her personal feelings about Nina, River had to concede that the woman's PR machine was impressive. Cameron's work had received glowing pre-exhibition reviews and the deluge of online and magazine interviews, accompanied by images of Cameron working at his easel in tight, paint-splattered T-shirts, had resulted in what was surely an incredible turnout for a debut artist.

Sly had escorted her past the security detail stationed at the entrance to the gallery and then left her while he directed the waiters struggling to get their trays of drinks around the room without damaging the exhibits. River moved out of the way of a couple trying to pass by her and scanned the crowded space in search of her girlfriends. It took a few minutes to spot Aku and the others in the crowd and she pushed her way across the room to join them.

'There you are! We were beginning to think you'd changed your mind,' Aku exclaimed after greeting River with a warm hug. 'Have you seen Cameron yet?'

River shook her head, unnerved at the prospect of running into her ex-boyfriend while at the same time hoping for a chance to congratulate him on his success. Ducking the question, River turned to greet the other two girls. The first one, a pretty, dark-skinned woman in a tangerine coloured minidress, squeezed River tightly until she laughingly freed herself.

'Oh my God, *Kukua*! I haven't seen you for so long!'

'Well, you're the one who disappeared on us,' Kukua replied. She took a step back and scanned River's white jeans and silky navy top critically. 'You've lost weight.' She looked River straight in the eye. 'Are things better with you now? We've really missed you.'

River swallowed the lump that had suddenly appeared in her throat and nodded, berating herself yet again for letting a man drive a wedge between her and her girlfriends.

'I'm fine – and I'm sorry I haven't been around. I've been such an idiot and it's so good to see my squad again.' She linked her arm through Aku's and beamed at the others. 'Believe me, you're not getting rid of me again.'

Half an hour and several false sightings of her exboyfriend later, River's nerves were stretched so tightly they could have strung a guitar. Feeling increasingly jittery, she stayed close to Aku and the girls as they wandered around the gallery, drinking wine, and jostling through the crowds to get close enough to see the exhibits. Many of the paintings were familiar but seeing them officially labelled and mounted below cleverly angled lights lent them a seriousness she had never given to the stack of canvases in Cameron's spare bedroom slash studio. River moved from picture to picture, struck afresh by Cameron's dramatic use of colour and shade. Listening to the hushed murmurs of admiration, she glowed with joyful pride at Cam's achievement, feeling a deep sense of gratitude his talent was finally being recognised.

'Oh my God!' Kukua had moved ahead of the other girls to look at the next painting when suddenly, wide-eyed, and almost screaming with excitement, she beckoned frantically to River. 'Quick, *come here!*'

Bewildered, River pushed her way through to where Kukua was pointing excitedly at the printed label next to a large oil painting. The exhibit was simply entitled '*River*' and she covered her mouth with her hand in shock. Then she gazed in wonder at the dramatic landscape of a river running through a forest of tall trees so thick with foliage they almost obliterated a scorching sunlit sky. The canvas was awash with colour; dark trees with dense green leaves and white foam-flecked waves in a river that blended vivid blues with shades of grey. The detail in the painting was stunning and captured the powerful force of the water as it crashed against huge rocks and boulders in its path and still flowed on.

River stared transfixed, taking in every detail even as her heart thudded painfully in her chest. *Is this how Cameron sees me?* The name given to the painting was no coincidence and it wasn't hard for her to interpret its message of a destructive river intent on its goal and heedless to the obstacles in its path and the beauty of its surroundings. She was so lost in the painting that the noise around her receded and it took her a few moments to realise the sudden silence was real.

River turned around just in time to see Nina with a glass in hand walking up to a dais with a microphone stand at the front of the room. As people moved forward, River shifted closer to Aku and the girls for a better view. Nina looked chic and confident in a black trouser suit with a silky silver-grey vest and a huge silver choker and, after quickly scanning the room, she beamed and plucked the microphone from its holder.

'Ladies and gentlemen, good evening and a very warm welcome. I'm delighted to see so many of you here this evening as we launch the first exhibition of an absolutely brilliant artist.'

She paused to survey the attentive crowd and her smile grew even wider. 'When I first saw this artist's work, I was so excited to meet him. I represent several talented artists but there was something so special, so... unique and – and compelling about Cameron's style that I knew immediately that I'd stumbled across an artistic *genius*.'

At the sound of a loud groan, Nina looked to her left and giggled. From where River stood, it was impossible to see who Nina was looking at, but River instinctively knew it was Cameron. Nina shook her head with a wry smile and continued. 'You've all seen his work on these walls, and you know I'm not exaggerating but I'm clearly embarrassing him so let me stop talking. Without further ado, I introduce our artist... *Cameron King!*'

To the sound of wild applause and raucous whistles, Cameron strode confidently to where Nina was waiting with arms outstretched. River's heart flipped wildly as she watched Cameron smile and raise his hands to acknowledge the cheers. *He looks beautiful.* She stared at him achingly, absorbing every detail of his well-cut dark suit and the crisp white shirt open at the neck. His hair was cropped lower than usual and his teeth gleamed white against his dark chocolate skin.

When Cameron hugged Nina and kissed her cheek, River felt a sharp pang as she remembered the news article Sefa had shown her speculating on the relationship between the artist and his agent. The pain was even more savage when Cameron began his speech by thanking Nina for changing his life. His words sounded so heartfelt there was an audible murmur of '*aah*' from the audience. Drowning in misery, River listened as Cameron went on to thank the gallery staff and single out Sly for his support. She craned her neck trying to locate her best friend and the sudden movement must have caught Cameron's eye because when she turned back, he was staring directly at her. Their eyes locked and she stopped breathing, vaguely aware that he had stopped speaking. The tense moment seemed to stretch on forever until Cameron wrenched his gaze away from hers.

There was further cheering and whistling when Cameron finished his speech, and he was immediately engulfed by a crowd of well-wishers. River was still struggling to catch her breath and bring her heart rate under control and she grabbed a glass of wine from the tray of a passing waiter and tossed back half the contents in one swallow.

'Well done,' Kukua grinned as she watched River visibly struggle to regain her composure. 'I don't know how you kept your cool.'

'For real!' Aku chipped in. 'Did you *see* the look on his face when he spotted you?'

* * *

The concrete wall River had chosen to perch on was feeling considerably less comfortable after fifteen minutes. She knew the girls would be wondering where she was, and she tried to persuade herself to go back to the party. After chatting briefly with Sly and taking countless pictures of Kwame in different poses in front of the paintings which had once hung on his restaurant wall, River had slipped away from her crowd, desperately seeking fresh air to clear her head.

Apart from the security guards and a few smokers chatting idly near the gallery entrance, River was alone. The gallery was tucked into a side road and other than the toots of car horns in the distance, the only sound was the chirping of crickets. The peaceful silence was a welcome relief from the hubbub of the gallery and she steeled herself to return inside. She hadn't yet seen all the exhibits and she wanted a final look at the painting Cameron had named *River*. She also had to complete the task she had set herself, which was to find Cameron, congratulate him on his success, and then finally accept they were over. Cameron might have been shocked to see her at the party but judging from the lingering looks he had exchanged with Nina, her former boyfriend had moved on beyond a doubt.

'I thought you'd left.' As if her thoughts had conjured him up, Cameron's deep voice came from behind her.

Startled, River wheeled around to find him standing behind her with his arms folded across his chest. He had discarded his suit jacket and rolled up his shirt sleeves and she couldn't help staring at him. Embarrassed at her lack of self-control, she hopped off the wall, belatedly hoping she hadn't dirtied her white trousers.

'No, of course not. It's just... it was, you know, a bit

hot inside so I thought I'd come outside for some air.' She cocked her head to one side curiously. 'Why are *you* out here? This is your night and I'm sure everyone inside wants to talk to you.'

Cameron shrugged. 'I'm not exactly much of a talker, as you might remember. Anyway, I've given so many damned interviews over the last few weeks I don't think I've got anything left to say.'

He sounded so disgruntled that River felt a smile twitching at the corner of her lips. Getting Cameron to promote himself had always been a challenge.

'That's not a good enough reason for you to be out here,' she pointed out. 'Whether you like it or not, *you* are the star of the evening and you should be in there networking with the art critics and influencers.'

He looked so alarmed that she burst into giggles. 'I'm beginning to feel very sorry for Nina!'

He laughed ruefully. 'Anyway, I'm glad you came tonight. I wasn't sure if you would. You've been such a huge part of my journey and I was hoping you would at least visit the exhibition at some point.'

'It looks *amazing*, Cam,' she said earnestly. 'Your paintings are really and truly stunning. From what I heard walking around in there, everyone is so impressed. I bet you sell every single one of them.'

His face lit up for a moment, and then he said quietly, 'I'm surprised Donald Ayo is comfortable with you coming here. From what I saw of him, he didn't strike me as someone who would want his woman taking an interest in her ex's career.'

River bit her lip and stared down at the manicured

toenails peeking through her strappy white sandals. Her immediate instinct was to salvage her pride by not correcting Cameron's assumption. But then she remembered what her father had told her that evening several months ago: *Don't mistake stubbornness for strength*.

She looked up and met Cameron's gaze squarely. 'I'm not with Donald anymore.'

He stared back, his face devoid of expression, and River sighed dejectedly. 'Listen, I was going to find you before I left this evening to say how truly and deeply sorry I am for how I behaved towards you. I got so dazzled by the prospect of making a ton of money and getting my dream house and I messed up everything with us in the process.'

'You must have liked him a lot to let him come between us,' Cameron said stiffly. 'I guess you can't help who you fall in love with, and if—'

'I wasn't *in love* with him,' River protested. 'I was *never* in love with him. Maybe it looked that way because we were photographed out a lot together, but I never slept with him!'

Cameron looked incredulous. 'So, wait, if you didn't love him, was it all just about his *money*?

'No, Cam, it was about me making *my* money. Yes, okay, he gave me some gifts and he even lent me his stupid car, but it was never about wanting him to finance me. I've always earned my own way, you *know* me!'

'I thought I did, until the day you put him before me and made *his* needs your priority.'

River fell quiet. 'I was wrong to do that and I've regretted it every single day since. Donald is very persuasive, but I'm the one who allowed him to convince me that spending time with him and his network of millionaires and celebrities would help build my clientele. I didn't realise until it was too late that what Donald really wants is control, which for him meant destroying my relationships. Including the most important one of all.'

Cameron looked sceptical and River exclaimed in despair, 'Cam, I promise it's the truth! I didn't need to tell you any of this, but I want you to know that I don't lie anymore.' She hesitated, remembering her job as an estate agent, and added candidly, 'Well, not to you at any rate.'

To her astonishment, Cameron roared with laughter, his shoulders shaking as he laughed so hard she could see tears. Wiping the heel of his hand across his eyes, he shook his head slowly from side to side. 'Jeez, River, why do you make it so hard to forget you?'

She smiled at him tremulously. 'So, you haven't forgotten how it was with us, then? You know, when – when things were good?' Under the dim street lights, Cameron's eyes were hypnotic pools of liquid darkness and River couldn't tear her gaze away.

'I remember everything about every day we've ever spent together,' he said in a low voice. For a moment they stood in silence with the insistent chirping of crickets as the only soundtrack to the rapidly thudding heartbeat inside her chest. Unable to hold back any longer, River opened her mouth to blurt out her feelings when a cheery voice broke into the still of the night.

'Oh, *there* you are, Cameron! I've been looking everywhere for you.'

River blinked in shock as Nina sauntered up to them and slipped a possessive hand through the crook of Cameron's arm. She stared at River speculatively for a moment and then turned her gaze on to Cameron. 'Hmm... why does it seem like I'm always having to break you two up?'

She tugged gently on Cameron's arm. 'The Arts correspondent from *The Daily Times* wants an interview with you.' She glanced at River with an apologetic smile. 'I'm sorry to interrupt but I'm going to have to steal him away from you.'

Without waiting for a response, Nina swept Cameron off, leaving River to watch helplessly as the couple disappeared through the doorway into the gallery.

Chapter 19

'River, I have a new client for you!'

River looked up at Harvey who was rubbing his hands together and looking incredibly pleased with himself. She put down the lease document she'd been browsing and gave him her full attention.

'Let me guess... another one of Jerry Andoh's friends wants us to sell their house?' she teased.

Notwithstanding River's firm belief in the power of networking, even she had been overwhelmed by the stream of friends and colleagues Jerry and Cynthia continued to send their way. Elated by the sale price River had negotiated on his behalf, Jerry was singing her praises to anyone who would listen. Cynthia, meanwhile, had taken to River like a mother hen to her long-lost chick and the combined power of the couple's contacts easily put Donald Ayo's celebrity pals in the shade.

Harvey chuckled and shook his head. 'No, not this time. I have an old friend who needs to view a property. He hasn't got a clue what to look out for and wants some guidance. I'd do it myself, but I've got a meeting with the Regency Bank people about that commercial property in Tema and so if you're not too busy, I'd really appreciate your help with this. We'll handle the purchase if he likes the house, so what do you say... 30 per cent of my commission to handle this?'

'Yes, of course,' River said absently, tossing the lease into her desk drawer. 'Where's the house?'

Harvey handed over a sheet of paper and she gave the address a perfunctory glance. 'What time should I get there?'

Harvey was already walking away, and he called over his shoulder, 'He's on his way now so it's probably best if you leave a-sarp.'

Shaking her head in amusement, River reached for her handbag and car keys. She checked her phone and grimaced. No texts or missed calls. Not that there was much chance of her missing anything considering she carried her phone everywhere in the hope Cameron might ring.

It had been over a week since the exhibition launch party and she'd relived their conversation outside the gallery countless times. But whenever she fantasised about what might have been had she admitted to loving him, the reality of Nina literally snatching her man away would rear its head and crush her dreams. As each day passed with no communication from her ex-boyfriend, the tiny secret flame of hope River had nursed of them somehow getting back together was finally flickering out. Cameron's continued silence reinforced her heart-breaking but inescapable conclusion that while he might have forgiven her, he had no desire to try again.

Dealing with the pain of rejection was even harder given that her ex was now the talk of the town. As River had predicted, Cameron's exhibition had attracted fantastic reviews and she couldn't escape the constant ping of excited WhatsApp comments from her friends. Even Sly, still riding high from being name-checked in Cameron's speech, had developed the annoying habit of pointing out to River – as if she needed reminding – how she had once dated the artist now trending on everyone's social media. Ignoring her stony looks, Sly bombarded River with snippets from the media reviews he'd collated for the gallery, just in case she was unaware Cameron had been named the sexiest artist in the country and his paintings were selling like hot cakes. As much as it hurt River to admit it, Nina was clearly proving her worth by getting Cameron the attention and rewards he deserved after his years of hard work and dedication to his art. After all, as River also conceded in her more generous moments, it wasn't Nina's fault that River had stupidly allowed herself to lose the best thing that had ever happened to her.

River slipped the phone into her bag, turned off her computer and walked out to the car park just in time to see Harvey driving off. She scanned the address he'd given her again and groaned in irritation. Her boss had been in such a hurry to get to his meeting he'd forgotten to give her the client's name.

* * *

River stepped out of her car and gazed approvingly at the modern, two-storey semi-detached house. With huge windows and a glass-enclosed balcony on the upper floor, it was ideally located less than twenty minutes' drive from the beach.

Assuming from the car parked in the driveway that Harvey's friend had already arrived, River manoeuvred her way past the vehicle to walk up to the house via a pathway of paving stones laid across a neatly tended lawn. The front door was slightly ajar, and she rapped the brass knocker firmly against the solid hardwood and waited. Having tried Harvey's phone several times to no avail while driving to the property, she still had no idea who she was supposed to be advising.

River was just about to knock again when the door swung wide open and she found herself face to face with Cameron. Like a rabbit caught in the blinding headlights of a fast-approaching car, all she could do was stare at him.

Cameron looked amused and was clearly enjoying her reaction. 'I see Harvey didn't let on that I'm your new client.'

'*How*—?' River broke off and shook her head, wondering if she had wandered into some parallel universe. *What the hell was Harvey playing at?*

'I never thought I'd see the day when you ran of words,' Cameron remarked before stepping back to wave her inside. 'Why don't you come in while you gather your thoughts. I could really do with your advice on this place.'

Struggling to process what was going on, River walked into the hallway with Cameron close behind her. She forced herself to gather her composure as she looked around the spacious open-plan layout. The large windows created a light and inviting atmosphere, but there was no sign of any furniture and it was clear the house was vacant.

'Well, what do you think so far?' Cameron interrupted her appraisal and she turned to him, baffled.

'I'm confused. Why are you even looking at a property when you already have a house?' She narrowed her eyes trying to work out what he was up to.

'You mean, I have a *rental*,' he corrected, sounding like a teacher schooling a slightly dim student. 'I have it on good authority that renting is a waste of money when you can own a property. Besides, my lease is up shortly, and I've decided not to renew it. It's time I found a house that doesn't turn women off.'

River flushed, but Cameron was already on his way to the living area and she meekly followed behind. The space was well laid out and with the right furnishings she could imagine it transformed into an elegant sitting room. She was suddenly conscious of Cameron staring at her as if trying to gauge her reaction and she raised an eyebrow in silent enquiry.

He gave a sheepish smile and folded his arms across his chest. 'Thank you for coming, River. I'm sorry I didn't ask you for help directly, but I was afraid you might find it awkward and refuse. After seeing this place last week, it hit me that buying a house is a big deal. Harvey seemed to think you wouldn't mind working with me on this and quite honestly, I wanted the best real estate broker in town.'

Having recovered from the shock of seeing Cameron, River forced herself to play it cool and sound nonchalant. After all, if he was mature enough to reach out for her help as a friend, the last thing he needed was the embarrassment of her throwing herself at him.

'Well, then you came to the right person,' she said lightly. 'What I've seen so far looks good. Where's the kitchen? That's always my deal breaker.'

'Over there.'

River followed his direction and opened the door to a large kitchen fitted with pale grey oak cupboards and grey and white marbled worktops. She walked around slowly, nodding in approval at the large utility space between the kitchen and the back door.

'It's very nice,' she said finally, peering through the window at a paved area behind the kitchen. 'They've done a good job with the layout and you've got enough room out there to pound your own *fufu*.'

She turned back to see Cameron's lips twitch in amusement. He made no comment and she sighed inwardly. It was a struggle to maintain a professional demeanour when all she wanted to do was pounce on the man. He looked ridiculously sexy in tight denims and one of his endless supply of white T-shirts and the mischievous twinkle in his eye was making it even harder to maintain her composure. Then she thought of Nina and wondered if the plan was for her to move in here with him. Reminding herself of the reason Cameron had asked for her, River took a deep breath and tried to focus.

'How many bedrooms are there upstairs?' she asked briskly. 'I'm guessing two.'

Cameron nodded without elaboration.

'Will that give you enough space? I mean, you own a lot of materials, not to mention your paintings—'

'Oh, yeah, about that. I want this to be a proper home and so my plan is to rent a space for a studio when life gets a bit calmer. In the meantime, I could use the formal dining room over there as a studio and put a dining table into the alcove bit at the end of the living room.'

'So, then, two bedrooms will be enough for you?' River persisted. 'You know, for your clothes, books and um… any guests?'

'I should think so,' he shrugged. 'Let's go up and take a look.'

River followed him upstairs, trying to control her pulse as she watched him take the steps in lithe, athletic bounds. When she reached the landing, Cameron immediately opened the nearest door and stood in the doorway while she inspected the empty bedroom and put her head around the door of the en-suite shower room.

'It's a good size and there's lots of wardrobe space. You know, especially if you need room for a lot of clothes...' She threw in the last comment offhandedly as she emerged to join him on the landing, half-hoping he would take the bait and let slip any plans for Nina to move in. When he shrugged without further elaboration, she nodded towards a door at the far end of the landing.

'I suppose that's the master bedroom?'

Cameron nodded with a teasing smile and River heaved a sigh, suddenly tired of playing games. The prospect of inspecting the room where he would be making love to another woman was absolute torture and she'd had enough.

'Okay, I know it's none of my business, but I *need* to know. Are you planning to move in here with Nina?' she asked baldly.

'Why do you need to know?'

'Please, Cam. Just *tell* me.'

He looked at her speculatively for a moment and then shrugged. 'That's not on the cards. I think you've got the wrong idea about Nina and me. You see, even if I was in love with Nina – which I'm not, by the way – I'm not her type.'

'Why the hell not?' River demanded; deeply, and illogically, offended on his behalf. 'You – you're *gorgeous*!'

He laughed and moved closer to her until they were only inches apart, causing River's heartbeat to accelerate rapidly. 'Well, I'm relieved you think so but trust me, Nina is very happily in love with Rachel.'

River was so mesmerised by his smile that it took a few moments for his words to sink in. Then her eyes widened, and she beamed, completely forgetting she was supposed to be acting cool.

'*Oh!*' she breathed with relief.

Cameron was watching her closely. 'So, you *do* care, then.'

She slapped his shoulder in exasperation. 'Of *course*, I care! I did everything but tell you so at your launch party! You haven't called me once since then and I thought *you* didn't want to know.'

'Come with me.' Cameron grabbed her hand and led her along the landing. He stopped in front of a large object covered in a white sheet propped up against the wall. He whisked the sheet away and River gasped as Cameron stood back to reveal the painting he had entitled *River*. Stunned into momentary silence, her gaze swung from the large canvas to its creator, and back again. Recovering her voice, she stammered in bewilderment. 'But – but Sly told me it's not in the gallery anymore which means it's been sold.'

'It was never for sale. I was just hoping you would come to the exhibition and see it. The truth is I couldn't get you out of my head, so I had to paint you out. Not that it worked,' he added ruefully. 'In fact, I don't think there's anything that will ever get you out of my head.'

River gazed in silence at the magnificent artwork and her eyes slowly filled with tears. 'It's *so* beautiful, Cam. Even though it shows what an awful, destructive person you think I am, it's still an amazing piece of art.'

Cameron sighed and shook his head. 'You know, River, you're a fantastic real estate agent but you'll never make an art critic.'

She frowned and blinked back her tears. 'What do you mean?'

'What I mean, my darling, is that the painting doesn't show you as destructive. Well, not *just* destructive, anyway... please don't look like that, I'm kidding!'

River opened her mouth, but he gently placed a finger on her lips. 'Listen to me for a minute. Yes, *of course* this painting represents how I see you. But what I see is someone strong and determined and who keeps going, no matter what obstacles get in your way. You're an incredible force of nature and I don't know anyone who has more discipline and focus when it comes to achieving their goals. I've always admired that about you even when I didn't like what it was doing to us. River, the truth is that you're the one who taught me to hold on to my dreams and have the courage of my convictions about being an artist.'

'But I didn't stick with you when you needed me, did I?' she said sadly.

Cameron shrugged and gave a wry smile. 'I didn't say you were perfect.'

He reached for her hand and looked deeply into her eyes. 'Listen, you're not the only one who messed us up.

Even if you had moved into my place like I suggested, the way things were going between us, it would probably have killed what was left of our relationship. I was way too selfish and self-absorbed instead of thinking about your feelings. Thanks to you, I knew I'd make it one day with my art but that didn't justify me putting you on the spot the way I did. Instead of making at least some changes to my lifestyle to prove I was serious about us, I just took for granted that we could carry on as we were and get married and have a family.' A flash of sadness crossed his face. 'I guess we both got caught up in our separate dreams.'

River looked down at her hand in his. 'You deserved better than the way I behaved, and I wish I had shown more faith in you.'

'River, you stuck it out with me for five *years,* so it wasn't as if you didn't try. I didn't appreciate how frustrated you'd become and when you tried to tell me, I got defensive instead of listening. You were right, my house *is* a dump and just looking around this property, I realised I should have moved years ago.'

'Cam, we've wasted so much time,' she whispered miserably, reaching for his other hand.

'Yeah, but I think we both needed the time to grow up. Look, it's taken us going through all this – this nonsense to realise just how much *we* matter.'

He grinned and suddenly he looked like an excited child. 'Come with me – I'm not finished yet!'

Before she could argue, Cameron led her across the landing to the master bedroom and flung open the door. River caught her breath and covered her mouth in shock.

The room was crammed with flowers. Colourful bouquets arranged in large glass vases set on the floor lined the four walls of the large empty room while a pile of red rose petals had been scattered in the shape of a massive heart in the middle of the floor.

Overcome by the heady scent of the fragrant blossoms and the utterly unexpected romantic gesture, River made no protest when Cameron gently led her to stand in the heart of rose petals. Then she gasped as he hitched up a trouser leg and dropped smoothly onto one knee.

'In the past, whenever I talked about marriage, I made it sound like it was something we should do to help you save for your house fund or keep your mother happy. But the truth is that marrying you would make me the happiest man on the planet. I love you, River Osei. Please marry me and I promise to do everything possible to make *you* the happ—'

Before he could finish, River dropped down onto the floor and threw her arms around his neck, sending them both tumbling onto the carpet of petals.

'You've just messed up my proposal!' Cam protested laughingly when River stopped kissing him long enough for him to speak.

'I can't believe you did all this for me!' she squealed in excitement. 'But I'm so confused! How did you set this all up?'

Cameron chuckled. 'Yeah, well, you can thank Harvey for that. He couldn't have been more helpful when I explained what I wanted to do, and he sorted everything out with the vendors and the keys. He kept insisting I propose *a-sarp* and muttered something about it being one in the eye for Donald Ayo. I think it's fair to say Harvey isn't that man's greatest fan.'

'Forget Donald Ayo. I definitely have,' River said firmly. 'Now, what were you saying before I interrupted you?' She giggled and stroked his face lovingly. 'I'm sorry I cut you off –you just looked so cute that I couldn't resist.'

She cleared her throat and put on a straight face. 'Okay, I'm ready. Now, ask me again!'

Cameron propped himself up on one elbow and caressed the curve of her cheek. 'I love you to the mountains and back, my crazy, tempestuous River. Will you marry me?'

She pulled him down and kissed him fiercely. 'Of course, I will,' she said. Then, suddenly anxious, she pulled back and looked into his eyes. 'Are you really, *really* sure about this?'

He kissed the tip of her nose gently. 'One hundred percent. There's no point in living the dream without the woman of my dreams.'

She smiled at him mistily and then snuggled against him. 'I love you so much, babe.' She was struck by a thought. 'Are you really going to buy this house or was all this just a ploy to get me here?'

Cameron shrugged. 'That depends on you. Do you like it? As far as I'm concerned, any house with you inside it is my home.'

She hugged him tightly. 'I don't know how I ever thought I could be without you. I don't care where we live so long as we're together but… about this house. It's very pretty and has nice features, but it's a bit small for a *family* home.' Her lips curved into a shy smile. 'What would you say to us putting our house funds together and buying a place with a couple more bedrooms which would be more... um, you know... family friendly?'

Cameron's eyes widened as he took in the implication behind her words and then he burst into laughter. 'River, you really are something else!'

Kissing her hard, he pulled her tightly against him. 'You know, I told you at the gallery that you're hard to forget, but what I didn't say is that you're also *very* easy to love.'

River raised her head and looked deep into his eyes for a moment before wrapping her arms around his solid strength, completely oblivious to the hard flooring beneath them. For the first time in forever, she didn't need a vision board to show what the future held for her and her gorgeous, loving artist. It had taken her time and cost her dearly to realise it, but she knew now beyond any doubt that Cameron was her heart and her home, and there was no house on the planet which could ever compete.

The End

If you enjoyed reading *River Wild*, please take a moment to write a review on Amazon, Goodreads, BookBub, or any other platforms you use.

Even if it's only a line or two, I'd really appreciate it!

Also in the Marula Heights series:
SWEET MERCY

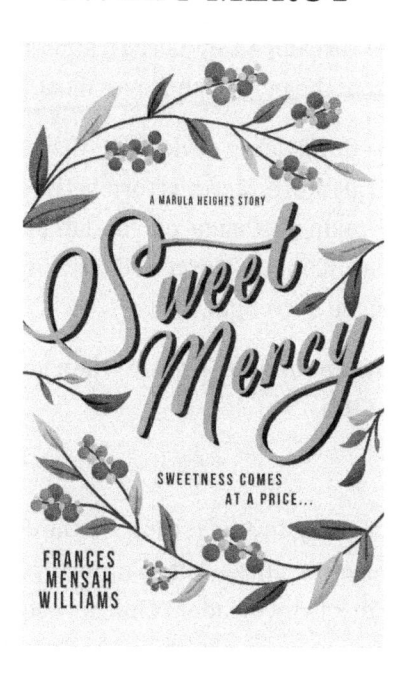

Sweetness comes at a price...

When sweet-natured Mercy married successful businessman and aspiring politician, Lucas Peterson, she abandoned her media career to focus on her husband and raising her son, Hakeem. But with the country now hurtling towards elections, Lucas's eye is on the ministerial position he craves within the Party and when Mercy's best friend, Araba – the niece of the Party leader – returns to Ghana, Mercy refuses to see what's obvious to everyone.

In a desperate bid to regain control of her life, Mercy reaches out to her friend, Max Bamford, a ruthless media boss with a reputation for uncovering corruption. Max's lifeline changes everything, but Mercy's hopes for a new beginning are threatened by Lucas's ambitions and risk the happiness of the person she loves most.

Armed with devastating evidence that can destroy Lucas's political future, Mercy is torn between protecting her son and taking revenge on his father. Faced with an impossible dilemma, Mercy will have to prove that sweetness can be a strength.

Available now on Amazon or free when you sign up to my Readers Club.

* * *

If you'd like to stay in touch (and be the first to know about new releases and events I'm involved with) you are welcome to join my Readers Club now and receive my free newsletter and future freebies… and your FREE copy of *Sweet Mercy*.

The Marula Heights novellas are companion stories to:

IMPERFECT ARRANGEMENTS

There are two sides to every story...

In the sun-soaked capital of Ghana, best friends Theresa, Maku and Lyla struggle with the arrangements that define their relationships.

Ambitious, single-minded Theresa has gambled everything to move with her loving husband Tyler from London to cosmopolitan Accra. But when shocking developments threaten their plans, they also expose the hidden cracks in their fairytale marriage.

Feisty Maku is desperate for professional recognition – and her dream white wedding. But how long can she wait for her laid-back partner Nortey to stop dreaming up pointless projects from the comfort of his local bar and stand up to his family?

Churchgoing Lyla married Kwesi in haste, and six years later she is desperate for a child. But while she battles a vicious mother-in-law, and her growing attraction to the mysterious Reuben, her husband has bitten off more than he can chew with his latest mistress.

Facing lies, betrayal, and shattered illusions, each couple must confront the truth of who they have become and the arrangements they have enabled. Against the backdrop of a shifting culture, each woman must decide what – and who – she is willing to sacrifice for the perfect marriage.

Available on Amazon and online retailers and from selected booksellers.

Praise for *Imperfect Arrangements*

'The queen of romantic dramas is back... this charming read is about the challenges which come with friendship, love, and relationships, and the search for that happily ever after.'
The Top 20 African Books of 2020, African Arguments

'Following three couples on the cusp of significant life changes, this charming romance... explores the difficulties of relationships at varying stages. Williams... weaves in vivid cultural details as she lifts the veil on the realities of marriage, the woes of infertility, and the strain of gender roles. Readers are sure to enjoy this uplifting work.'
Publishers Weekly

'The beautiful, tropical backdrop is the ideal setting for this tale that is crammed with realistic, complex characters. It is an easy-to-read exploration of modern love and relationships. I very much enjoyed this brilliantly written novel.'
Dorothy Koomson, bestselling author of *The Ice Cream Girls* and *Tell Me Your Secret*

'In *Imperfect Arrangements*, Frances Mensah Williams slices through the lives of three couples and presents a witty, true, and, sometimes, heartbreaking portrayal of married life in Accra, Ghana.'
Ayesha Harruna Attah, author of *Harmattan Rain* and *The Hundred Wells of Salaga*

'This novel is a celebration of sisterhood. You'll cheer on Theresa, Lyla and Maku as they navigate life in modern Accra, dealing with difficult bosses, feckless husbands and dubious mother-in-laws. You won't want to put the story down till it ends.'
Chibundu Onuzo, author of *The Spider King's Daughter* and *Welcome to Lagos*

For more about Frances Mensah Williams and her books:

Visit my website at www.francesmensahwilliams.com

Connect with me

Twitter: @FrancesMensahW
Facebook: www.facebook.com/francesmensahwilliams
Instagram: francesmensahw

Other Books by Frances Mensah Williams

Fiction

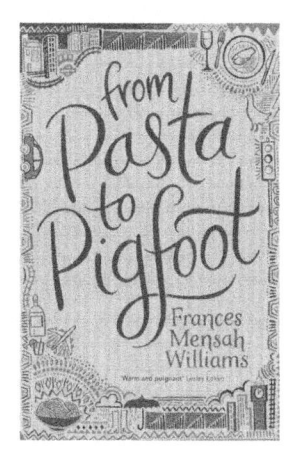

From Pasta to Pigfoot

On a mission to find love, a disastrous night out leaves pasta-fanatic Faye's romantic dreams in tatters and underscores her alienation from her African heritage. Leaving London to find out what she's missing, Faye is whisked into the hectic social whirlpool of Ghana and into a world of food, fun and sun to face choices she had never thought possible.

From Pasta to Pigfoot: Second Helpings

Pasta fanatic Faye Bonsu seems to have it all; a drop-dead gorgeous boyfriend, a bourgeoning new career and a rent-free mansion to call home. But with friends shifting into yummy mummy mode, a man with no desire to put a ring on it, tricky clients, and an attractive and very single boss, things are not exactly straightforward. Faye returns to sunny Ghana, but life doesn't always offer second chances.

Non-Fiction

I Want to Work in Africa: How to Move Your Career to the World's Most Exciting Continent

A practical, invaluable guide to the African job market, the industries and professions in demand, how to put in place a winning strategy, write a compelling CV, make the right connections, and find a job in Africa that builds on your career and talents. Illustrated with personal stories and full of practical advice from recruiters and professionals who work in Africa.

Everyday Heroes: Learning from the Careers of Successful Black Professionals

A collection of interviews with sixteen professionals with different careers including law, accountancy, music, publishing, medicine, banking and architecture. These 'everyday heroes' talk about what it takes to succeed in their careers, their own influences and the life lessons they have learned along the way.

Printed in Great Britain
by Amazon